"Barr . . ." Vick . . . struggling to talk . . . intoxicating distra . . . caresses. "I have to talk to you, to explain—"

"To explain why you're going to say *no* again?" His voice was rough with desire, but tinged with a hint of wryness.

"To tell you that I haven't been entirely honest with you . . ."

She felt a subtle change in him, a wary tightening that suddenly reminded her he could be ruthlessly harsh as well as tenderly loving.

"In what way?" he asked, his voice tautly balanced, as if it could tip toward love—or anger. . . .

RENA MCKAY
is an American writer currently living in the far west. The setting for her well focused novels reflect her love for her native country and add an extra dimension to her sensitive and finely drawn characters.

Dear Reader:

I'd like to take this opportunity to thank you for all your support and encouragement of Silhouette Romances.

Many of you write in regularly, telling us what you like best about Silhouette, which authors are your favorites. This is a tremendous help to us as we strive to publish the best contemporary romances possible.

All the romances from Silhouette Books are for you, so enjoy this book and the many stories to come. I hope you'll continue to share your thoughts with us, and invite you to write to us at the address below:

Karen Solem
Editor-in-Chief
Silhouette Books
P.O. Box 769
New York, N.Y. 10019

RENA McKAY
Valley of Broken Hearts

Silhouette Romance

Published by Silhouette Books New York

America's Publisher of Contemporary Romance

Other Silhouette Books by Rena McKay

Bridal Trap
Desert Devil

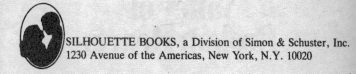

SILHOUETTE BOOKS, a Division of Simon & Schuster, Inc.
1230 Avenue of the Americas, New York, N.Y. 10020

Copyright © 1983 by Rena McKay

Distributed by Pocket Books

ISBN: 0-671-57239-3

First Silhouette Books printing August, 1983

10 9 8 7 6 5 4 3 2 1

Map by Ray Lundgren

America's Publisher of Contemporary Romance

Printed in the U.S.A.

Valley of
Broken Hearts

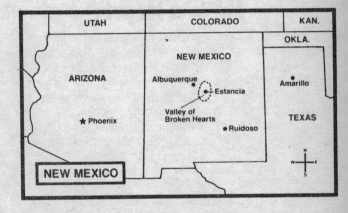

Chapter One

They had tried to make the evening just like old times. They had eaten Aunt Verla's golden crisp fried chicken, potato salad, lemonade, banana cream pie. They had chattered and laughed and reminisced, brought each other up to date on who had married whom, who had a houseful of children and who had a career. The old house still lacked air conditioning, and the portable fan by the screen door made a familiar rumble as it moved the hot July evening air around the kitchen.

But Vickie Thornton was painfully aware that this wasn't just like old times. Uncle Ed's place was conspicuously empty. Aunt Verla, when she thought no one was looking, had a hurt, faraway look in her eyes and an absent-minded habit of twisting the wedding ring she still wore. Kathy's laugh, always so bubbly and infectious, was forced now, and her face and figure had lost that deliciously rounded, cuddly look that high school boys had once found irresistible. Outside, the noise of traffic was more raucous than Vickie remembered it being on this suburban Amarillo street.

Finally, Vickie asked the question that had hovered unspoken all evening. "Have you heard anything about the kids, Kath?"

Vickie had been reluctant to ask the painful question, but now she had the unexpected feeling that Kathy had been waiting to pounce on it, that everything up to now had been some tedious but necessary preliminary. Kathy carefully set down the stack of plates she had started to carry to the sink. Her hands were trembling.

"I know where they are now. He's taken them to the family's ranch in New Mexico."

"Kath, that's wonderful! Now that you know where they are, you can take some definite legal action. . . ."

Kathy's smile was bleak. "Your faith in the legal system is touching. But misplaced." The bitter statement was so uncharacteristic of the irrepressibly optimistic girl Vickie had always known that she was shocked.

"But surely there's something you can do," Vickie protested. "People, even *fathers*, can't just go around stealing children. It seems to me I was reading not long ago that there are some new federal laws about child snatching. . . ."

This time it was Aunt Verla who interrupted, her voice as shockingly bitter as Kathy's had been. "Laws work best for the person who can afford the highest-priced lawyer."

"Oh, Kitten, everything is in such a mess." Kathy's lower lip trembled, and she caught it between her teeth. Blinking back tears, she picked up the stack of dishes again and carried them to the sink.

Vickie already knew the general facts of the situation, of course. Kathy had married Ric Chandler when they were both attending college near El Paso. Kathy was studying home economics, and Ric was majoring in agriculture, but his real ambition was to be a race-car driver. Both had dropped out of college to follow Ric's dream. According to Kathy, however, the dream had turned into a traveling nightmare. Benji was born in Florida, Susan in Kansas.

Finally, Ric decided to admit his failure at auto racing and face his obligations. He gave up racing and went to work as a car salesman in an East Coast city. Even this didn't strengthen the marriage. More problems surfaced. Finally, Kathy filed for divorce. Kathy's mother, Vickie's Aunt Verla, went up to help out while Kathy tried to pull her life together. Ric showed up at the house late one afternoon while Verla was taking care of the kids. He was pleasant and calm, saying he had run into Kathy downtown and had come to pick up the kids so they could all go out for pizza together. Without hesitation, Verla had let him take Benji and Susan, hoping his visit meant they might all get back together again as a family. That was some six months ago, and Kathy hadn't seen her children since. Neither had there been any word except for one terse phone call from Ric a few days later saying that he had the children, they were fine, and he intended to keep them.

"But surely when your divorce came up for a hearing and you told the judge what had happened . . ."

"I dropped the divorce when I moved back here with Mom." Kathy's voice sounded wooden. "I knew Ric could afford better legal help than I could, and I was afraid of what might happen in court since he already had the kids. As far as I know, we're still married."

"Then maybe what you ought to do is see a lawyer about starting divorce proceedings again and get a judge to issue a legal-custody order."

"Kitten, I don't want to hear any more legal gobbledygook from some lawyer or listen to some pompous judge's opinions or go through years of legal battling while my kids grow up without me." Kathy sounded infinitely weary. "Benji's fifth birthday is next month. I want to bake a birthday cake for him and hold him in my arms. I want to feel Susan's grubby little fingers tugging at my hair." Kathy closed her eyes and swayed. A tear slipped out from beneath her lashes. "I just want my kids. I love them."

Vickie leaped up to steady her cousin and guide her to a chair. She felt helpless. "But if you don't think the legal system will help you, what can you do?"

Kathy straightened as if a fine wire had tightened in her spine. "I can do the same thing Ric did. I can just take them. And *then* I'll start talking to lawyers and judges."

Vickie shook her head. "Kath, honey, I just don't think that's the way. It's surely illegal. . . ."

"Is loving and wanting my kids illegal?" Kathy flared. "Was what Ric did legal—or right?" She took a deep breath, struggling for control. Then she looked directly at Vickie. "Kitten, we've never really asked much of you. . . ."

Vickie caught her breath, green eyes widening. It was true. For years Kathy and her parents had shared with and given to Vickie and asked practically nothing in return. "You want me to help snatch the kids back?"

"No, not directly. As you pointed out, it's probably illegal, and I wouldn't ask that of you." Kathy tilted her head and added reflectively, "Though what is *legal* and what is *right* aren't necessarily the same thing."

With more animation than she had shown all evening, Kathy went on to explain that through some friends she had located a man who specialized in helping parents in just such a situation as this. Her eyes had a glow of hope, as if a light had been turned on inside her. Vickie had heard of people such as this man Kathy was talking about. "Custody vigilantes," they were sometimes called. Whether they were good or bad seemed to depend on which side of the custody battle you happened to be on. It was this man, Kathy went on, who had learned that the children were definitely on the ranch in New Mexico. He had, in fact, spent several days in the area, but he had concluded there was simply no way to snatch the children while they were on the ranch.

"You mean they're being held *prisoner* there?" Vickie gasped.

Kathy shook her head, a flutter of impatience in the movement. "Oh, no, nothing like that. It's just that the ranch is so big, and they can see a car coming for miles, and there are always ranch hands or someone around. But this man made inquiries at a couple of little towns nearby and learned that sometimes the kids come to town with Ric or his mother. He thinks the kids *can* be snatched sometime when they're off the ranch. But no one happened to bring them into town while he was there, and I couldn't afford to pay him to hang around waiting for days or weeks. He says what he needs is some kind of advance notice about when Benji and Susan will be off the ranch so we could make definite plans to rescue them."

"I don't quite see where I fit in." Vickie managed an encouraging smile in spite of a sinking feeling inside.

Kathy walked over to a drawer and returned with a sheet of paper. It was a photocopy of part of the want-ad section of a newspaper—an Albuquerque, New Mexico, newspaper, Vickie noted swiftly. One classified ad was circled in red. It was for an experienced secretary-bookkeeper to work on a ranch in the Estancia Valley area. Salary open, commensurate with abilities and experience, plus board and room. A phone number followed.

"Kitten, I wouldn't ask it of you if it weren't so—so awfully important. And I wouldn't ask you to quit a job to do this. But since you *are* between jobs, anyway . . ." Kathy's voice was pleading, but there was something else in her eyes, a determination, a conviction that she was in the right.

"You're saying that this ranch is where the kids are," Vickie said slowly to make certain there was no misunderstanding. "You're saying I could take this job and then give you and your friend advance notice about when the kids were to be taken to town or somewhere. And then the two of you could snatch them."

Kathy nodded as calmly as if Vickie had outlined no more than an afternoon's shopping schedule. "He says if he can have twenty-four hours' notice, he'll drop everything else to help me. And giving us advance notice is *all* you'd have to do," Kathy emphasized. "Just one phone call to tell us where the kids are going and when. We'll do the rest."

Vickie shook her head doubtfully. She didn't want to turn her cousin down. She owed Aunt Verla and Uncle Ed and Kathy so much. And yet . . . "Hon, I just don't see how it could work. I've met Ric. And the kids, too, of course. And this ad is ten days old. The job is probably filled by now."

One by one Kathy demolished Vickie's objections. She was coolly logical, no longer the "fluff brain" Uncle Ed had once called her in exasperation. Mother love and loss had obviously matured her. She pointed out that when Vickie had last seen the kids, Benji had been a toddler, Susan little more than a baby. They couldn't possibly remember her. There was a slight possibility Ric would recognize her, but it was remote. He hadn't seen Vickie since she was in high school.

"And let me tell you, you've changed since then," Kathy said, nodding her head significantly as she appraised Vickie's slim but rounded figure and silky cloud of black hair. No longer could her figure be described, as it once had been by some unchivalrous adolescent boy, as "shaped like a two-by-four board with funny bumps."

"But my name. . . ."

"Kitten, I doubt if Ric ever realized your last name was different from mine. And if he did, he's never going to remember that the name was Thornton. And I'm absolutely positive he never heard your first name as anything but Kitten."

Kitten. Vickie's name had undergone a metamorphosis over the years. Born Victoria Catherine Thornton, she had been called Cathy because her mother was already Vickie. Then, after her parents' death and her going to live with Aunt Verla and Uncle Ed, there had been nothing but confusion with both a Cathy and a Kathy in the house. Her name had been shortened to Cat for a while, but Aunt Verla was aghast at that. So Uncle Ed turned it into Kitten, even though, with her skinny, wiry body, defensively antagonistic manner and tomboy ways, she was anything but kittenish. The name had stuck, however, until she was working and out on her own. Now she was Vickie.

Kathy wrapped up Vickie's final argument. "If you called and found the job already filled—well, that would take care of that."

Vickie studied the two faces watching her so hopefully, their eyes clinging as if she held the only life line in a sea of despair. The kids surely needed their mother, and Vickie owed Aunt Verla and Kathy so much. . . .

Vickie had been born in southern California. Her father was a publicity agent, and her parents were always involved in a busy social whirl of parties and promotions and openings and events. The gay whirl came to an end when they were killed in a car accident following a party. Alone and bewildered, Vickie was sent to Amarillo, Texas, to live with her only living relative, her mother's sister Verla, whom Vickie had never met. Vickie knew she must have been a thoroughly unpleasant addition to the household at first. She was scared and uncertain, somehow feeling that she would be betraying her parents if she accepted and returned the love these good people offered, and she hid her feelings behind a prickly barrier of hostility and rebellion. But in spite of her abrasiveness, Aunt Verla and Uncle Ed had treated her with firm but loving kindness. Kathy, three years older than Vickie, had uncomplainingly shared her room and belongings with this small hostile stranger, and eventually her generously good-natured, infectiously bubbly personality proved too much even for Vickie's determined hostility to resist. They truly became sisters more than cousins, though they more or less lost touch after Kathy's marriage. Vickie took a short business course after high school, then went to work in the office of an Amarillo construction company. The company expanded rapidly, and when they moved their headquarters to Shreveport, Louisiana, and offered Vickie an excellent job there, she accepted. The company's expansion had proved too rapid, however, and when the economic crunch came, the company had collapsed like a punctured balloon.

As Kathy had just pointed out, Vickie was definitely "between jobs" just now. There was nothing to keep her from taking a job, albeit a necessarily temporary one, in New Mexico. She really wanted to aid Kathy, but she couldn't help feeling there must be some better solution than this one. Yet she had only to look at Kathy's gaunt, drained face to know that her cousin was hovering on the edge of some sort of collapse.

In the end, it was Aunt Verla who pushed Vickie off

her knife edge of indecision. "I miss my grandchildren." The brief statement, so soft Vickie had to strain to hear it, was more eloquent than any impassioned speech. "You two and Benji and Susan are all I have left. And it was so much my fault. . . ." She looked down quickly, but Vickie saw the gentle, faded eyes brimming with tears. And the plain golden wedding band went around and around.

Aunt Verla felt responsible, Vickie realized. It was she who had been taking care of the kids when Ric stole them, handing them over to him without a protest. The pain on Aunt Verla's face was more than Vickie could bear.

She picked up the photocopy of the classified ads and crossed the room to the wall telephone hanging beside the kitchen counter. "I suppose Ric is the person I'll have to talk to about the job?"

Vickie had never been particularly fond of Ric, though she hadn't really disliked him until he had taken the children. Privately, she had considered him a little immature, but she could understand what Kathy saw in him. He was darkly handsome and had a certain daredevil charm. Until now, Vickie hadn't realized that he came from what was evidently a rather well-to-do family.

"Oh, no." Kathy looked slightly shocked at the idea of discussing the job with Ric. "You'll have to talk to Barr."

Vickie already had the phone to her ear, her finger poised over the dial. She dropped the phone to her shoulder and turned to look at her cousin. "And just who is *Barr?*"

"Ric's older brother. He runs the ranch. He runs *everything* when you get right down to it. Sometimes I think Ric and I might still be married if it weren't for

Barr." Kathy paused, head tilted pensively. "Or maybe he'd never have married me in the first place if it weren't for Barr."

"Kath, you're not making much sense." Vickie felt more bewildered by the moment.

Kathy momentarily caught her lower lip between her teeth to stop its trembling. "I was so much in love with Ric, and I thought he was in love with me, too, of course. But later, when we had so many problems, sometimes I wondered if he had married me just to spite Barr and prove that Barr couldn't run his life. I always had the feeling the whole family disapproved of me."

Vickie replaced the phone on the hook. "I think perhaps you'd better tell me a little more about this family so I'll know exactly what I'm walking into," she said slowly. She caught Kathy's nervous glance at the clock. "Don't worry. I'll call even if it's midnight," Vickie assured her. "We won't worry about disturbing the Chandlers after what they've done to us."

Aunt Verla stood up suddenly. She looked pale and worn. "I think I'll just run on up to bed while you two discuss this."

After she was gone, Vickie and Kathy settled at the table with fresh cups of coffee, leaving the dishes stacked in the sink. Another change, Vickie thought. She had never known Aunt Verla to go to bed with dirty dishes in the house.

Murmuring vaguely that there really wasn't all that much to tell about the Chandlers, Kathy went on to tell quite a bit. There were four children in the Chandler family: Barr, the oldest; twins Niles and Nancy; and Ric, the "baby of the family." Their father had been killed when Barr was only fourteen. Their mother ran the ranch alone until she was bedridden for months after her back was badly injured when she was thrown from a horse. At sixteen, Barr quit school and took over running the big ranch.

"And all that power turned this Barr into some kind of tyrant?" Vickie speculated.

Kathy frowned. "Evidently. But they have this kind of—of fierce family loyalty, even when they're hardly speaking to each other. Barr was dead set against Ric's car-racing career. Once Ric got pretty badly hurt in a race crackup. I didn't notify his family because he said not to, but somehow the very next day Barr turned up at the hospital. And believe me, Barr made sure Ric had the best of everything."

"And all was forgiven?"

A ghost of a smile touched Kathy's face. "Not exactly. They growled at each other, and Barr gave Ric hell for being stupid enough to race cars, and Ric told him to mind his own damn business. But all the time you could feel this—this bond between them, that the family was *there* for each other when the chips were down." There was reluctant admiration in Kathy's voice. "All that family loyalty is great when you're on the inside, but when you're on the outside . . ." She drew a slashing line across her neck. "And I'm definitely on the outside now." She gave Vickie a slanting look of warning. "And so are you. If you do get the job, don't ever forget that. When you do battle with one Chandler, you take on the whole family."

"A little like our family?" Vickie asked lightly.

Kathy's answer was meaningful. "I hope our family has that kind of loyalty."

"What about Mrs. Chandler? Is she still bedridden?"

"Oh, no. I met her only a couple of times, but she's one of those terrifyingly competent women who can do anything." Kathy's mouth twisted in a grimace. "I had the impression that she does things like single-handedly round up and brand a hundred cattle before lunch, collect a half million dollars for some Albuquerque charity in the afternoon and then whip up a fancy dinner for forty in the evening."

Vickie smiled at Kathy's sour exaggerations. "And you're asking innocent little *me* to walk into this situation? A tyrant of an older brother, an intimidating matriarch . . ."

"And two little kids who need their mother." Kathy's heartfelt comment ended the brief moment of lightness.

Vickie walked to the phone, wiped nervous hands on her jeans and dialed the long series of numbers long distance required. A softly accented female voice, not young, answered. Vickie explained the reason for her call. The voice asked her to wait a moment, and then a male voice came on the line.

"Hello. Barr Chandler speaking."

A shivery tingle shot through Vickie. The voice of the enemy, unexpectedly deep and rich.

"Hello. I'm calling about your advertisement in the Albuquerque newspaper for a secretary-bookkeeper. Has the position been filled?" Her breath caught, and she was uncertain whether she was hoping it had or hadn't been filled.

"It was filled a couple of days after the ad first appeared."

"Oh." Vickie's relief was mingled with a thud of disappointment as she saw Kathy's questioning eyes fastened hopefully on her.

"She lasted eight days. I fired her yesterday."

"Oh!"

"It turned out that she was considerably more interested in cowboys than in bookkeeping." Barr Chandler spoke with wry good humor, but there was a bite to his tone that suggested he had not been in a good humor when he fired the girl. If you didn't do the job you were hired for on the Chandler ranch, obviously you didn't last long. Vickie found herself wondering what Barr looked like. He sounded younger than she had expected after Kathy's unflattering comments. And there was that richness, almost a warmth, to his voice that she found disconcerting.

"The job is open again, then?"

He didn't answer directly. "Tell me about yourself, Miss . . . ?"

"Thornton. Victoria Thornton." Vickie went on to describe the extent of her experience with the construction company and her office skills and qualifications. She explained how she happened to be available and looking for a job now. "I'm sure there are important differences between construction and ranch bookkeeping," she added, "but I believe the basic skills should be transferable."

"And what did you do before you were employed by the construction company?" The question sounded casual, as if he were fully impressed with her qualifications.

"I've been with them almost four years." Vickie was inwardly congratulating herself. This was going to be easy. "Before that I was in school."

"I see. How old are you, Miss Thornton?" he added offhandedly.

"Twenty-two."

"I see," he repeated. There was a brief, meaningful silence. "I was hoping to find someone more—ah—mature."

Vickie felt a flare of anger at the suddenly condescending note in his voice. She had let her guard down, and he had led her neatly into a small trap. "Maturity is not necessarily a matter of years, Mr. Chandler."

His retort sizzled back across the line. "I'm not interested in providing another man-hungry, cowboy-crazy girl with the opportunity to conduct a husband-hunting expedition on my time and at my expense."

"You needn't worry about that with me, Mr. Chandler," Vickie snapped. "I've just ended two years of a bad marriage, and I can assure you I am *not* interested in acquiring another husband, cowboy or otherwise."

There was another small silence after the brief, fiery exchange. Out of the corner of her eye, Vickie saw Kathy's mouth drop open in astonishment at the blatant lie about a former husband. Then Kathy grinned and silently clapped her hands in gleeful applause, appreciating that Vickie was doing everything she could to get the job. Where had the wild story about a bad marriage come from? Vickie wondered. She wasn't above fibbing to help her desperate cousin, but for a moment she hadn't even been thinking about Kathy. She'd just wanted to say something devastating to puncture Barr Chandler's arrogant assumption that she was a man-hungry husband chaser simply because she wasn't what he considered "mature."

"Actually, then, it's *Mrs.* Thornton instead of Miss."

"Well, no." Vickie's hand felt sweaty clutching the telephone. "I use my maiden name. I didn't want anything of his." She was suddenly determined not to miss out on this job and chance to aid Kathy. She had never been "man hungry" or gone on a "husband-hunting expedition" in her life, and she didn't like being accused of it now. "I don't want anything from any man," she added frostily for emphasis.

Unexpectedly, he laughed, a warm chuckle that just as unexpectedly sent a tingle through her, as if a small jolt of electricity had raced across the telephone lines and through her body. "You sound as if you should be more than a match for a couple of my cowboys who see themselves as that macho type in the cigarette ads, irresistible to any woman."

"Am I to infer that perhaps your former 'cowboy-crazy' secretary was not totally to blame for whatever happened?" Vickie kept her voice cool and lofty.

"Perhaps." The word was noncommittal, but there was an undertone of held-back laughter.

Vickie had a panicky feeling that she was losing control of the conversation, and she made a frantic effort to regain it. "I'd like to know a little more about the job, please," she said crisply.

He explained the duties. The ranch had a certified public accountant in Albuquerque who handled quarterly financial statements and corporate and personal tax returns. The ranch secretary did day-by-day bookkeeping, payroll, ranch correspondence, record keeping on the registered cattle and horses and whatever other general office work might come up. She would also be expected to help Mrs. Chandler with some social duties and correspondence.

Vickie felt an unexpected jolt. *Mrs. Chandler.* Was he referring to his mother, or was Barr Chandler married? He certainly wasn't *flirting* with her over the phone, but she was almost certain she detected a note of speculative interest. And that, she realized with a small tremor, was something she would certainly have to nip in the bud. The last thing she could afford was to get romantically involved with Barr Chandler.

His next words, however, were crisp and businesslike, as he asked where he might contact her former employer for a reference. And then Vickie found herself entangled in another dangerous snare as he asked, "Your employment records are under your married name, I presume?"

"Well, no." Vickie's mind searched frantically for some plausible explanation for that discrepancy. "I married after I was already employed there, and I—uh —preferred to keep my own name. It's not uncommon

21

for a woman to do that today, you know," she added defensively.

"Perhaps your marriage would have worked out better if you hadn't been so stubbornly independent."

Vickie gasped at the outrageous remark. He had no business making remarks about her personal life! Then she had to laugh ruefully at herself. Here she was getting all worked up over a derogatory remark about a marriage that didn't even exist! Carefully, she forced a cool control she really did not feel into her voice.

"I'm sure you'll find my references satisfactory."

"I'll check them," he agreed. "Now, about salary . . . ?"

He left the words dangling, and she suddenly realized that he was going to make her name a sum. Oh, very crafty, she thought scornfully. He probably figured that way he could strike a better bargain with some woman desperate for a job. No wonder he wound up with a husband hunter.

Recklessly, Vickie named a salary above what she had been earning at the construction company. Kathy made frantic negative signals with her head and lowering motions with her hand.

If Barr was surprised, he was too controlled to show it. "That's a considerable sum, Mrs.—Miss Thornton. Are you worth it?"

"You won't know unless you hire me."

He laughed again, and she knew that her impulsive gamble had paid off. He had more respect for a woman who knew her own worth than one who downgraded herself. But again his husky, almost intimate laugh sent that distracting tingle through her.

"Where may I reach you after I've checked your references?"

The question froze Vickie to the phone, and she groaned inwardly. She'd been so desperate to erase that gaunt look of despair from Kathy's face that she'd gone into this without getting her act together. Now she stumbled through a disorganized and unlikely story about planning to leave Shreveport because her job was over, giving up her apartment and staying with friends for a short time. Finally, she asked if she could just call him back in a few days. Just when she thought it was all over, she had to come up with yet another created-at-the-moment explanation in answer to his curious question about how she had happened to see an ad in an Albuquerque newspaper.

She hung up the phone and sagged limply against the wall. She felt drained, as if she had been under interrogation for hours, though the clock said that only a few minutes had passed. She had been clutching the phone so tightly that her hand was cramped around it.

Kathy rushed over and hugged her gleefully. "You're going to get the job, Kitten. I just know you are!"

"Don't get your hopes up," Vickie warned. The sight of some trace of the old vivacious Kathy warmed Vickie's heart, but it frightened her, too. Kathy had her hopes soaring so high now. What happened if Vickie failed?

Kathy danced around, pulling Vickie in a circle with her as if they were children. "Oh, Kitten, you were terrific! 'I don't want anything from any man!'" she said, mimicking Vickie's tart retort. Her eyes danced, too, bright with some of her old mischief. "I knew you could do it!"

"I haven't done it yet," Vickie warned again. She dropped into a chair, feeling strangely warm and shivery at the same time. How many times in the space of that one conversation had she come close to getting entangled in her own lies? That wild story about having been married. The mix-up about her name. The weak story to explain why he couldn't call her. Mentally, she waded through the conversation again, searching for pitfalls. There was no way he could tell that she was calling from Amarillo, not Shreveport—was there? Would something come up about her "marriage" when he contacted the construction company for a reference? If she got the job, could she even remember all the fibs she had told on the phone?

A trickle of perspiration splashed between her breasts, and she suddenly felt an unpleasant queasiness that came from something more than sheer nerves. She hated being deceptive, telling lies, getting out of the entanglement of one story by telling another. She was basically a scrupulously honest person, once astonishing both her Shreveport roommate and a prospective buyer when she honestly admitted that the car she was trying to sell gulped oil like a kid downing soda pop. But she had no choice about being devious now, she reminded herself. It was the only way she could help Kathy and Aunt Verla and partly repay them for all they had done for her.

"Did he say anything about the kids?" Kathy bubbled on. "Such as maybe you'd be expected to watch them sometimes or something? But of course he wouldn't do that." Kathy laughed ruefully at herself. "That's silly, isn't it? I'm so excited I'm hardly thinking straight."

"Kath, how old is Barr Chandler?" Vickie asked.

"I'm not sure. Early thirties, I suppose. Why?"

"When you were talking about him earlier, I had the impression he was older. But on the phone he sounded —well, younger." She didn't add that he had also sounded disturbingly attractive. "Is he married?" she added casually.

"Not unless some girl managed to rope and tie him in the last few months. Not that half the ranchers' daughters in New Mexico haven't tried, I'm sure. He's attractive enough," she added grudgingly.

"Does he resemble Ric?"

Kathy shook her head. "They really don't look much like brothers. They're both tall and have that same lean, rangy build, but their coloring is different, and Barr is much more . . ." Kathy paused, but instead of finishing the physical description Vickie was curiously awaiting, she added enigmatically, ". . . intimidating."

She gave Vickie another impulsive hug. "You'll see what I mean when you meet him. Because you're going to get that job. I know it. And I'm going to get my kids back!"

Kathy went on up to bed, but Vickie lingered in the kitchen to wash the dishes and try to relax her quivery nerves. She wished she could share Kathy's certainty about the success of this venture. Alone in the silent, old-fashioned room that held so many memories, the scheme suddenly sounded preposterous, totally unworkable, utterly implausible. She could think of a hundred things that might go wrong, and at the top of the list was the possibility that Barr Chandler might somehow discover her real purpose for being on the ranch. Instinctively, she knew that even though Ric was the children's father, Barr Chandler was the real adversary.

He had been personable on the phone, wryly good-humored, masculinely self-assured. There had been a certain challenging excitement about matching wits with him, and his husky, intimate chuckle had hinted at a certain appreciation of her spirit and independence in spite of his disparaging remark about her "marriage."

But Vickie knew things about him that hadn't come across on the phone, and she didn't doubt for a moment that in a crisis that threatened people he loved, Barr Chandler could be chillingly ruthless.

Chapter Two

The Estancia Valley of New Mexico ran north and south, a broad, flat plain banded by the Manzano and Sandia mountains on the west, rolling gently into the vague blue line of the Pedernal Hills on the east. The dry clumps of grass on the treeless grazing land looked sparse to Vickie, but the cattle roaming there were fat and frisky. There were a few tilled fields and the occasional green jewel of an irrigated alfalfa field. The scattered ranch houses were marked by windbreaks of trees, and windmills stood as lonely sentinels against the immense blue sky.

Vickie wished she were seeing it all under different circumstances, when she didn't feel so churned up and apprehensive. When she had called the ranch a second time, steeled to talk to Barr Chandler, she had been informed by a crisp but not unfriendly female voice that she had the job. Mrs. Chandler, Vickie assumed. She had made a rush trip back to Shreveport to terminate the lease on her apartment and pick up her things. She had talked on the phone to the man Kathy had hired to help retrieve her children and been briefed on the basic plans.

And now here she was, looking up at an enormous sign arched over a gravel road leading off to the west.

The foot-high wrought-iron letters spelled out the name *Chandler*. Nothing else. Just Chandler, as if the ranch were a kingdom unto itself. A kingdom with Barr Chandler as king, she thought, summoning a certain scorn to keep herself from being too impressed.

She drove under the arch, bumping over the cattle guard that marked the property line. The road arrowed straight across the flat land toward a distant cluster of buildings and trees. Kathy was right about one thing, Vickie thought as she glanced in the rear-view mirror. Anyone approaching the ranch could be seen for miles. A banner of dust behind the car marked every inch of her progress.

At first, Vickie thought no one noticed when her car pulled into the yard, but then she realized that the Sunday-afternoon sleepiness of the scene was deceptive. A handful of barking dogs announced her presence, and a man peered out from under the jacked-up pickup on which he was working. A curtain moved at the window of a double-width mobile home. The strum of a guitar and then hearty male guffaws came from a bunkhouse. The main house was set off at a distance beyond these buildings, which were evidently living accommodations for the ranch workers.

Vickie approached the main house, feeling a strange mixture of apprehension and anticipation, curiosity and nervous excitement. The low, sprawling building of rich, cream-colored textured stucco accented with stone and dark wood and broad expanses of glass, had a quiet elegance emphasized by almost formal landscaping. The door opened before she rang the bell. An Indian woman, her mahogany face lined with age but timelessly beautiful, said in a soft voice that both Mrs. Chandler and Barr were away for the day, but they were expecting her. She would show Vickie to her room.

Vickie was annoyed. This was the second time she had braced herself for an encounter with Barr Chandler, and again he had eluded her. Of course, it was really Ric Chandler she should worry about first, she reminded herself. There was always the possibility that he might recognize her.

The room was pleasant, simple without being severe. One wood-paneled wall, the others white, a surprisingly luxurious rust-toned carpet underfoot. Private bathroom, dark walnut furniture and a generous closet. The window looked out on a swimming pool that glittered turquoise in the sunlight. Vickie was tempted to ask the Indian woman, who said her name was Doñela, if she might go swimming, but she decided against it. She didn't intend to meet Barr Chandler for the first time clothed in nothing more substantial than the three pink triangles of her bikini.

She started to unpack, then uneasily decided against that, too. Surely she wouldn't be living here in the main house with the family. If things went right, she might not even be on the ranch more than a few days, and she needed to be ready to grab her things and run on a moment's notice.

She paced in front of the window, took a shower to wash away the day's travel grime and paced by the window again. If it weren't that she was certain Barr Chandler didn't consider a new secretary all that important, she might think he was deliberately making her wait to unnerve her—to prove he was the all-powerful boss. Or king.

Doñela returned and said she had prepared a small supper. A single place was set for Vickie at a breakfast bar. By that time, dusk had fallen, and Vickie had decided, with both disappointment and relief, that she evidently was not going to meet any of the Chandlers today.

She was savoring the juicy hot roast beef sandwich when she heard doors opening, male voices and then the husky laughter that was already familiar. She tried to swallow, but her throat suddenly clamped shut, and her mouth was embarrassingly full when the two men walked through the arched doorway.

Vickie's eyes rested only momentarily on Ric Chandler. In a strictly handsome face contest, Ric might have a slight advantage, but next to Barr, Ric's dark good looks appeared superficial, a little trite or stereotyped. Barr Chandler had chestnut hair tracked with sun streaks, tiny lines fanning gray-green eyes, a finely chiseled mouth and an unmistakable air of strength and authority. For a moment, Vickie had the awful feeling that those penetrating, sage-colored eyes saw right through to who and what she was, but then the mouth flashed a welcoming smile as he strode toward her. At that point, Vickie knew Ric had no advantage at all in the looks department.

"I hope you're Victoria Thornton. I spent Friday going over the books, and at the moment I'm not sure if the ranch is solvent or not."

Somehow Vickie managed to force the roast beef down and mumble something appropriate. Kathy had said that Barr was "intimidating," and Vickie had finally settled on the mental image of a rough cowboy type hiding his lack of education under a thin veneer of money and running the ranch by brute force. Except for the rugged cowboy build, Barr didn't match that mental image at all. There was a dance of good humor in his eyes when he smiled. He wore tailored tan slacks and a crisp white shirt with cuffs turned back over golden-tan forearms. His only concession to western dress was a pair of quietly expensive western boots.

Vickie was so engrossed in meeting Barr that for a few moments she forgot the danger in encountering

Ric. She tardily realized that she had passed the first test with flying colors when Ric acknowledged Barr's introduction to her with little more than a nod in her direction and a glance at his watch.

"I think I'll run over and pick up the kids before Carol puts them to bed there."

Questions flashed through Vickie's mind. Who was Carol? Where were the kids? She ached to know, but for now she had to be content that there was not even a puzzled haven't-I-seen-you-somewhere-before glance from Ric. Vickie felt a bubbling excitement as Barr sat down beside her. This just might work, after all! Or was it something other than the prospect of success that made her heart bounce erratically? she wondered, suddenly suspicious of herself. She was sharply aware of Barr's basic maleness, an attribute that had never before jarred her right down to her frosted toenails.

"Sorry we weren't here when you arrived. We spent the day down at the race track at Ruidoso."

"Car races?" Vickie asked in surprise, considering what she knew about Barr's attitude toward Ric's car-racing career. She caught her error immediately. She wasn't supposed to know anything about Ric—or racing—or kids! She had let her guard slip, reacting to Barr's imposing virility like some starstruck groupie.

"Spoken like a true city girl. Here, Victoria Thornton, when we talk about races, we mean *horse* races." His voice was loftily teasing. "Quarter-horse races, to be specific. But we didn't do too well today. Our gelding only ran third."

Vickie tried to ignore a rush of warmth at the sound of her name coming from his lips. Doñela brought him coffee and a heaping plate of food. Vickie made a determined attempt to concentrate on her own food.

"Mom decided to spend the night at Ruidoso," Barr

called to Doñela. "She's driving up with Niles and Serena tomorrow. The trainer is coming, too, to pick up another filly, so better count on a houseful."

"Where is Ruidoso?"

"Hey, you pronounced the name right. It makes the natives furious when tourists mangle the name." He smiled at her and helped himself to a generous forkful of hot beef and gravy. "It's down in the south central part of the state. We flew down for the day," he added as casually as Vickie might report that she had run to the supermarket back home.

She had heard an airplane a few minutes before the two men arrived at the house, but until now she hadn't connected the sound with their arrival. She suddenly felt almost overwhelmed. She, Vickie Thornton, was going to triumph over the Chandlers with all their planes and race horses and wealth and power? She was going to outwit Barr Chandler, who, for whatever unknown reasons, made her breathlessly aware of her own vulnerable femininity in contrast to his male strength? The idea suddenly seemed ludicrous.

She set her knife and fork neatly on the half-eaten food and slid unsteadily off the bar stool. She had intended to stay until Ric returned with the kids so she could tell Kathy how they looked, but suddenly she felt an overpowering need to escape and gather herself together.

Barr's arm shot out and steadied her as she stumbled slightly getting off the high stool. "Hey, you've hardly eaten anything."

"I—I guess I'm just tired from the trip."

"Doñela showed you your room, didn't she?"

"Yes, but I assume it's just for tonight. I mean, I saw the quarters for the other ranch workers. . . ."

"I don't think we dare put you in the bunkhouse with

31

the men," Barr said, "though I'm sure *they* wouldn't object. In fact, I might be tempted to move into the bunkhouse myself."

His chiseled mouth curved with a hint of laughter, and his voice was lightly teasing, but he was still holding her upper arm, and a certain gleam of appraisal in those gray-green eyes was more speculative than laughing.

"Where . . ." Vickie felt as if that firm but warm grip were on her brain rather than her arm. She could feel the back of his encircling hand against the outer curve of her breast. "Where did your other secretaries stay?"

"Our foreman's wife kept the books for several years. She and her husband lived in the foreman's house, of course, but they've bought a little ranch of their own now. Miss Husband Hunter stayed in the same room you have."

"So I will be staying here in the main house—permanently?" The final word came out in a strangled croak. How could she talk about *permanently* when she was only planning to step in, do her underhanded duty and sneak out?

"More or less. But it isn't a life sentence."

Vickie smiled weakly, uncertain whether he was making fun of her or warning her that she might go the way of the cowboy-crazy husband hunter. "Well, I—I think I'll just go to bed now. I'll see you in the morning?"

"Doñela will show you where the office is located."

Vickie had planned to telephone Kathy that night, knowing how anxious her cousin was for word about her children. They had arranged that Vickie would always call collect so that no incriminating evidence would appear on the ranch phone bill. Now Vickie decided to postpone the call until tomorrow night. She really had no information to provide yet, and she didn't

32

know the location of a safe phone. There was a telephone on the breakfast bar, but that was far too public.

The office was located at the end of one wing of the house. Vickie was there early the next morning, but Barr was already sitting behind a cluttered oak desk. He looked more the cowboy today, dressed in jeans, blue chambray work shirt and scuffed boots—little different from the men who worked for him, but there was no mistaking who was in charge. He briefly went over the books with Vickie and told her that he wanted to take her into Albuquerque to talk to the accountant before the next payroll was issued. He said he usually spent only part of the day in the office, but he would be there all day today in case she encountered problems.

The books weren't all that bad. "Miss Husband Hunter" must not have spent all her time chasing cowboys. Vickie doubted that she would have any problems getting the records in order and bringing them up to date. Barr was on the phone frequently, often long distance, talking to a stockyard in Phoenix, ordering a machinery part from Albuquerque, selling a rather large block of Wall Street stock. He was crisply businesslike with Vickie, more preoccupied than unfriendly.

Good, she thought. Keep this strictly business. That would make everything easier. Last night, at the breakfast bar, she had been uneasily aware that a danger she had never anticipated might lurk here. She had never expected that she might feel a certain—what?—for Barr Chandler. Something shivered through her as she eyed the lean slant of his hips beneath the taut Wranglers when he walked to a file cabinet.

Curiosity, she assured herself. She was merely curious about him. But there was a twinge of something

33

else when Vickie answered the phone, a young female voice asked for Barr, and his voice changed subtly as he talked to her, his words interspersed with husky laughter. He had swiveled his chair to face away from her, so she couldn't hear everything, but she caught his intimate "See you tonight, then" before he hung up. So, Barr Chandler might be cagey about getting "roped and tied" in marriage, but he wasn't averse to an occasional dalliance with a rancher's daughter.

Ranch workers came into the office several times during the day with various bits of business. Vickie was uncertain whether this was normal or whether they were finding excuses to look her over. One in particular, a real macho type with mustache and a God's-gift-to-women swagger, lingered longer than seemed necessary. He made a point of telling her that he was really a rodeo cowboy, not "just a ranch hand." With the other men, Vickie was friendly in a businesslike, reserved way, but with this ego-inflated one she was distinctly icy. Barr seemed preoccupied with a livestock report, but Vickie thought she saw his mouth twitch in amusement. Ric came in once, a grease slash on his cheek, to talk about truck parts.

Vickie was hoping to see Benji and Susan at lunch, but they evidently ate early. Later, however, she heard childish squeals and laughter and made an excuse to rush to her room so she could look out at the pool. There were a half-dozen children in the pool, but Vickie had no trouble picking out towheaded Benji. He was so brown and wiry and energetic! And Susan was the image of her father, with dark hair and incredibly long eyelashes. Once Benji raced by the window so close that Vickie could have reached out and grabbed him. She felt a rushing ache of sympathy for Kathy, existing without those two. She was glad she was alone and unobserved when she first saw the kids. She must *never* reveal any affection or personal interest in them.

A big Lincoln, followed by a pickup and empty horse trailer, pulled into the yard in late afternoon. Immediately, the house took on a hustle and bustle of activity. Phones rang, delicious scents drifted out from the kitchen and the pool sounds changed to adult laughter. Vickie felt a little awkward as her work day ended. Some social event was evidently planned for this evening. Was she supposed to eat in the kitchen and keep out of sight?

Barr settled that by saying casually that there were a few extra people around, so dinner would probably be buffet style. She could meet the family then.

Vickie assumed that Barr wouldn't be there since he had evidently made a date for the evening. She was reluctant to step into some social gathering where she knew no one, and she decided to ask Doñela if she couldn't just fill her plate in the kitchen and take it to her room. Later, after everyone was in bed, she planned to slip into the office and call Kathy.

Vickie changed her mind when she heard an older woman's firm but affectionate voice telling the children that they had to put on their good clothes because company was there for dinner that night. She wanted to report every possible detail to assure Kathy of her children's well-being, and this would be another opportunity to see them. She had no idea what to wear, but settled on a pale-yellow sun dress with spaghetti straps and matching jacket and brushed her dark hair back from her face in a slightly more sophisticated look than the usual loose tousle of curl.

The house seemed full of people when Vickie finally gathered up her courage and went out. She glanced around the room looking for the kids, but before she located them, her eyes met Barr's. He was looking at her differently than he had all day, as if he had mentally shifted gears after working hours. Or was perhaps seeing her in a different perspective.

"And who is this gorgeous creature?" a big male voice suddenly boomed.

Barr stepped forward. Until then, Vickie hadn't even noticed a leggy blonde standing beside him. "I'd like everyone to meet the ranch's new secretary-bookkeeper," Barr announced. "Victoria Thornton." He went on to identify for Vickie the various faces around the room, starting with the owner of the booming voice, Hale Wardlow. "Don't let the distinguished appearance fool you," Barr added. "Hale is your friendly neighborhood lecher." The big, middle-aged man smiled agreeably.

"And my uncle." The blonde rolled her eyes in exaggerated despair. She was Lou Ann Wardlow. The voice on the phone, Vickie assumed.

Vickie nodded and smiled in response to the introductions, filing away for future reference the names she thought she'd need to know. Niles was a brother, half of a twin set, Vickie remembered, though no one mentioned that. Serena was his wife. They lived in Phoenix, Arizona, where Niles managed the feed lot on which the ranch cattle were finished for market. Mrs. Chandler was surprisingly tiny and fragile looking, considering Kathy's intimidating description. There were others, the horse trainer and his helper and some friends from Albuquerque, also returning from a weekend at Ruidoso.

"You've already met Ric, of course," Barr finished. "And these are his children, Susan and Benji."

The kids looked adorable sitting at a little table set up just for them, their feet dangling off the floor. Susan wore a pink froth of ruffles, and Benji was manly in little blue pants and a white shirt. Ric had his long legs stuck under the table so he could eat with them. Carefully, Vickie didn't let her eyes linger too long.

The evening went pleasantly enough, though Vickie had perhaps more male attention than she really wanted. The distinguished-looking lecher seemed determined to live up to his reputation, and the horse trainer followed Vickie around as if she were a prize filly. Vickie treated them as she had the cowboys in the office; she was friendly but reserved. Barr kept his distance, though Vickie felt his eyes contemplating her thoughtfully more than once. The blonde appeared to have taken root on his arm.

The conversation was bright and fast moving. Everyone was interested in the horse races at Ruidoso and in one special ranch-bred filly that had been nominated to run in some particularly important race called the All-American Futurity. Vickie gathered that Mrs. Chandler had hand raised the filly after its dam died and started its training herself.

"What's her name again, Amanda?" someone called to Mrs. Chandler. "I want to be sure to get my money down on her."

Mrs. Chandler made an exaggerated groan. "I'm embarrassed to say. Here she had this tremendous bloodline and all these illustrious ancestors, and her name should reflect that. Instead, my son . . ." She cast a dark glance toward a smiling Barr. "My son registered her as *Amanda's Baby*."

Laughter followed, and Vickie gathered that Mrs. Chandler wasn't really too displeased with the name. Then the big, distinguished-looking lecher bore down on Vickie again.

"How do you like our valley so far, Miss Thornton?" he boomed. There was no having a quiet, private conversation with Hale Wardlow. On second thought,

Vickie decided she probably should be grateful for that. "May I call you Victoria? Or Vickie?"

"Vickie is fine," she murmured.

"Our valley has quite a history, you know," Hale announced. He went on to give her a fairly detailed account of how the valley had been settled by homesteaders who prospered because soil and climate were just right to make the area the "Pinto Bean Capital of the World." But then times changed, the devastating winds came and the ideal climate for beans went away, never to return. The homesteaders went broke and moved away, dreams and hopes blasted by drought and wind. "They called it the 'Valley of Broken Hearts' then," Hale said.

Vickie was impressed. She had the feeling that Hale Wardlow wasn't quite the burlesque figure he let himself be made out to be, and he really knew his subject. But his niece just wrinkled her pert nose.

"Is that what that old story is really all about? And here I thought 'Valley of Broken Hearts' had something to do with the amorous activities of the Chandler men." Her voice and sparkly blue eyes were impish, and everyone laughed.

The gathering broke up around eleven o'clock. Some of the people were evidently staying the night; some weren't. Vickie went to her room, trying to douse a smoldering curiosity about whether Barr was taking Lou Ann Wardlow home. She changed into a brief nightie and covered it with a blush-pink velour robe. The night was chilly at this altitude even though the afternoon had been warm.

She waited restlessly until the house settled into silence and no lights gleamed from any windows she could see from her own, then moved swiftly down the dimly lit hallway, intent on reaching the office. In dismay, she saw a crack of light coming from beneath the door. Could Barr possibly be in there at this hour? She was standing outside the office, wondering if she could have left her desk light on, when the door opened and the light went off. Just as quickly, it flashed back on again as Barr realized someone was standing in the hallway.

He peered at her with more curiosity than suspicion. "What's this?"

"I—I just happened to think that I hadn't recorded some of the off-road fuel usage correctly." She was surprised at the ease with which she improvised. Did she really want to become the type of person who fibbed so fluently?

He leaned one arm against the doorjamb, head tilted. The backdrop of light touched his chestnut hair with a sheen of gold, and in silhouette, his lean frame, stripped of nonessentials, had a raw, elemental masculinity. "I know I must have sounded like an ogre of a boss on the phone, but I really don't expect you to work twenty-four hours a day." He sounded on the edge of annoyance.

"You're working," she pointed out. The words were merely to fill space while she tried to compose herself. Part of her shaky feeling came from the close brush with disaster. What if he had caught her talking on the phone to Kathy about the kids? But part of her discomfort was something else. She felt disturbingly exposed in the feminine robe, with so little underneath, even though the robe actually covered her more thoroughly than her daytime clothing. The soft velour suddenly felt lushly sensuous against the almost naked skin beneath it. She touched the zipper to make sure it was closed tight to her throat. She suspected that he noticed the nervous gesture.

"I'm finished working now. I was just thinking I might have a drink before I went to bed. Will you join me?"

"No!" The explosive rejection was out before she realized that it sounded a little foolish, as if she thought he was inviting her to his bed rather than merely suggesting a drink. "I mean—no, thank you," she added stiffly.

"You're very good at that," he said unexpectedly.

"Good at—what?"

"Keeping men at a distance. I watched you do it all day. And tonight, too."

"You made your opinion of husband-hunting secretaries rather clear!"

He laughed. "You mustn't take my remarks quite so seriously. You're allowed to smile at the men." He paused, his own smile lazy. "We aren't entirely off limits."

Vickie's heart began to beat faster. *We* aren't entirely off limits. Merely an accident of speech or something more significant? She felt a dangerous intimacy hovering in the air. The silence of the sleeping house . . . the dim light . . . the midnight hour. The chance meeting suddenly felt intimately clandestine.

"We'll have a glass of wine. It will help you sleep." The softness of his voice did nothing to dispel the feeling of intimacy. "You must be having trouble sleeping or you wouldn't be worrying about fuel usage at this hour. Come. . . ." He touched her shoulder lightly to turn her in the opposite direction.

Vickie jerked away so violently that her out-flung hand struck the opposite wall of the hallway. The sound reverberated with astonishing loudness, like a small boom of distant thunder. She had the awful feeling that people might come running to see what the commotion was. But no one did, and they just looked at each other, Vickie's luminous green eyes wide. She clutched her numb fingers with her other hand.

"You're a little jumpy," he observed finally.

Again, she had overreacted. Why? Because just for a moment she had thought he was going to turn her into his arms. Now she felt utterly and completely foolish, reading something seductive into a polite invitation for a drink, jerking away as if she thought he intended to snatch her up and carry her off to his bedroom. Of course, his voice was soft; everyone else was sleeping.

Resolutely, she lifted her head and thrust her hands into the deep pockets of the robe, determined to show him *she* wasn't attaching undue importance to a shared glass of midnight wine. "A small glass of wine would be fine."

He snapped off the office light again. "Down the hall and across the living room."

She walked briskly, quelling an urge to tiptoe along the dim, silent hallway. His light touch guided her across the expanse of the living room and then into a darkened room that was flooded with soft lamplight when he touched a switch. The room was a large, comfortable den, with built-in stereo and television and a casual grouping of sofas and chairs. The feeling of dangerous intimacy was stronger than ever. Vickie determinedly tried to banish it with banal conversation.

"You have a lovely home."

"Thank you. Make yourself comfortable." He walked around behind a small, mirrored bar, casually flicking another switch that sent the soft strum of a classical guitar floating through the room.

Vickie sat in a chair a little apart from the others, trying not to be conspicuous about avoiding the love seats and sofas. Barr brought amber wine in a glass whose long stem was twisted in a graceful spiral. To her consternation, he then perched comfortably on the wide arm of her chair.

The wine was faintly sweet and felt as if it flowed directly into her veins, filling them with a languid warmth. The warmth combined with the soft, wild throb of the music and golden lamplight to create a romantic, clandestine atmosphere; it seemed as if they were lovers meeting for a secret midnight rendezvous.

"I should have the books brought up to date within a few days. And then I think the files should be reorganized." Vickie felt a panicky necessity to talk about business in order to avoid a dreamy urge to let her head drop back against the cushion and give herself up to the wine and the music.

Barr chuckled lightly. "Vickie, I told you you don't have to think about work twenty-four hours a day. You don't mind if I call you Vickie, do you? You told Hale Wardlow it was all right."

But the sound of her name coming from Hale's lips didn't feel like a warm-honey caress, she protested silently. But all she said was "Everyone calls me Vickie."

"Who is 'everyone'?"

"Oh, coworkers and friends . . ."

"Family? Boy friends? Ex-husband?"

Were his finger tips lightly brushing her hair? No, she surely must be imagining that. She tried to concentrate on what she had told him on the phone about her family and "marriage," but at the moment her mind wouldn't focus clearly enough to remember. "Everyone," she repeated evasively.

He reached down and caught her fingers playing nervously with the stem of the wine glass. "Did you bruise your hand when it hit the wall?"

She resisted the urge to jerk away again, but he felt the initial withdrawal.

"Does a man's touch really disturb you that much now?" he asked softly, rubbing her fingers lightly with his. "In the hallway, when I touched you, your eyes looked like those of a wild doe caught in a spotlight." His hand moved up to cup her chin and turn her face to his. "They still do."

"I'm not—disturbed." It was as large a lie as any she had yet told.

"You're not what I expected, you know. On the phone you sounded so hard and sure of yourself."

"I'm sorry if I've disappointed you!"

"That isn't what I said." His thumb slid up to caress the corner of her mouth as his eyes roamed her face. Instinctively, her hand went to his wrist, but if she had intended to push his hand away, her subconscious had other plans. Her finger tips took in the touch as if each nerve ending were exquisitely sensitized to magnify the contact. Fine, soft hair over warm skin, taut sinew and muscle around a solid core of bone . . . Her finger tips against his pulse threaded their heartbeats together until they throbbed as one.

"You—you're not what I expected, either."

"The way your voice trembles when you say that, I'm not certain if it's compliment or accusation."

Neither was Vickie certain. There was a hint of soft laughter in his voice but a dark smolder of something else in his eyes. Why, oh, why, wasn't he what she had expected? Arrogant, aloof, rough, crude, all the things an enemy should be. Not warm and laughing and so powerfully, self-confidently virile that he could afford to be tender. The combination loosened a wild jumble of unfamiliar yearnings within her and wakened her to a sweet, fiery longing to be kissed.

Somehow he had slid into the soft depths of the chair with her, and his body cradled hers. Her slippers, frivolously impractical bits of high-heeled fluff, dangled for a moment and then dropped to the floor with soft thuds. He ran his hand lightly over the bare curve of her foot, a small touch that was strangely erotic. She could feel the hard muscles of his thighs beneath her legs, but she didn't know if the thunderous heartbeat was his or her own. One breast rested against his chest, and his male heat seeped through the velour robe to envelop the breast in intimate warmth. His finger tip traced the outline of her lips, and then his mouth moved toward hers with a slow, deliberate certainty.

With a strength born of the fear of her own shocking weakness in letting this go so far, Vickie threw herself to her feet. She couldn't—absolutely must not—let herself get involved in any way with Barr Chandler. She must never forget that she was here for one purpose only, and she must be ready to walk away at any moment without a backward glance.

"Vickie . . ."

Vickie didn't wait to hear whether he intended apology or angry accusation or seductive persuasion. She was all too wildly aware that at this moment she was vulnerable to any or all.

"I meant what I told you on the phone! I don't want anything to do with men—any man! I—I've had all I ever want of that!"

She stumbled toward the hallway, flung the door open and raced headlong in barefoot flight toward her room, uncertain if she was fleeing from him—or herself.

Chapter Three

Next morning, no word passed between Barr and Vickie concerning the midnight incident in the den. Barr was his usual efficient, slightly preoccupied self.

Vickie might have thought she had imagined the whole thing were it not that she found her slippers neatly lined up beside her office desk. The champagne bits of bedroom fluff looked incongruous in the office setting. Vickie unceremoniously kicked the slippers under her desk where they couldn't be seen until she could return them to her room at lunch time. She was uncertain whether Barr's method of returning the slippers was meant to be discreet or whether he was subtly making fun of her. Her impassioned speech and headlong flight struck her as a little melodramatic now.

She was very much aware, however, that there was nothing at all melodramatic about the hazards of involvement with Barr and that the risk was real indeed. He was dangerously attractive, both in a very physical, sexually magnetic way and in some other way that Vickie couldn't quite define. She must be on constant guard that she never let some attraction for Barr, physical or beyond, distract her from her purpose here.

Barr didn't return to the office after lunch, and

Vickie managed a surreptitious phone call to Kathy. She reported that the kids were tan and healthy and energetic. They had the pool to play in, playmates their own age among the ranch workers' children and an abundance of affection and attention from all members of the family. By now, Vickie knew that "Carol" was a ranch hand's wife who occasionally took care of the pair and that they hadn't been off the ranch since Vickie's arrival. She added that at breakfast she'd heard Ric promise the kids that he'd saddle up their ponies for a ride this evening.

"You make it sound as if they're better off there than they would be with me," Kathy said reproachfully. "Ponies and pools and everything."

"Oh, Kath, I didn't mean that." Vickie was instantly remorseful that she hadn't used better judgment in what she told Kathy. "I just wanted you to know they're *okay*, that they're not being mistreated or ignored or anything. Kids need their mother more than they need ponies and pools." But they need their father, too, a conflicting voice within Vickie echoed, and she couldn't doubt but that Ric's love for the kids was just as strong as Kathy's.

"Okay. I know." Kathy's voice cracked, as if it took all her effort not to break into sobs. "Just—call me again as soon as you can. And make it the kind of call we're waiting for."

"I'll try," Vickie promised.

By midweek, Vickie was beginning to realize more than ever how difficult it was going to be to keep that promise. That Wednesday, Benji and Susan were away from the ranch all afternoon, but Vickie didn't know a thing about it until dinner time when they were chattering excitedly about the birthday party they'd been to in Estancia. Mrs. Chandler had dropped them off at the party and gone on to a church board meeting. It would have been a prize opportunity. How was Vickie ever going to learn of plans *ahead* of time?

On Thursday morning, Barr announced that he had an appointment with the accountant in Albuquerque that afternoon and wanted Vickie along for a brief consultation. They left immediately after lunch. Barr and the accountant held a short private discussion, and then the accountant went over various aspects of the bookkeeping procedures with Vickie, making sure she understood New Mexico payroll deductions, since she had come from out of state.

Vickie assumed they would return to the ranch immediately afterward, but Barr casually asked if she would like to visit Albuquerque's "Old Town" area.

The afternoon spent wandering through Old Town was an unexpected and delightful treat. Jewelry and other Indian wares were spread outdoors under a covered walkway, owners lounging alongside and agreeable to bargaining over prices. There were dozens of shops selling everything from inexpensive souvenirs to lovely hand-woven Navajo rugs, bronze sculptures and fine oil paintings. Vickie was especially entranced with the small Mexican tiles hand painted with graceful flower and geometric designs. They were surprisingly inexpensive, and she purchased several, planning someday to frame them. She was further surprised when Barr made a couple of purchases of his own, a small leather belt for Benji and a kachina doll for Susan. They bought chocolate chip ice cream cones and licked them while sitting on wrought-iron benches in the shady central square. Across from the square was the lovely old San Felipe de Neri church, built around an adobe church first established in 1706.

Barr was good-humoredly tolerant of Vickie's inability to pass up even one of the interesting little shops and cheerfully waited while she agonized over a choice between two pairs of delicate silver and turquoise earrings. In a word, Vickie would have described his behavior as *gallant*.

Afterward, Barr suggested they might as well stay in town for dinner and a movie. Despite a faintly guilty feeling that she was consorting with the enemy, Vickie readily agreed, and the evening was as companionably enjoyable as the afternoon had been. Barr, she decided, had evidently taken to heart her impassioned speech about men, although some small part of her mind warned that he might be outwitting her, lulling her into a false sense of security, to get what he wanted. And just what *did* Barr want? The dangerously tantalizing possibilities sent a quicksilver tremble through Vickie and brought a disturbing memory of the unfamiliar reaction of her body to the hard masculine touch of his in the den.

There were only a few moments that were less than pleasant all day. In the crowded lobby of the theater after the movie was over, Vickie suddenly realized that the strap of her handbag was being deftly slipped off her shoulder. She gave a small cry as the thief darted away through the crowd. In two swift strides, Barr had him. Barr's two-handed grip on the man's shoulder and elbow looked little more than casual, but Vickie knew from the way the man's face suddenly went pasty white that the grip was far more ruthlessly painful than it looked.

It was all over in a few moments, the thief smoothly delivered to the manager's office without fuss. Vickie felt shaken as Barr guided her out to the car, his firm grip gently protective now. Vickie had conflicting feelings about the upsetting incident. One side of her appreciated Barr's quick, ruthless reaction. It made her feel safe and protected, almost—cherished. But now she had gotten a glimpse of the side of Barr's character that Kathy had evidently seen, the harshly intimidating man who wouldn't hesitate to act with brutal ruthlessness when necessary. It was a potent, shivery reminder that all that tight-lipped fury would someday soon be directed at her when he figured out her devious purpose for being on the ranch.

At the ranch house, Vickie thanked Barr for a lovely day. She felt a certain self-consciousness about entering the same house with him after the "date" was over, and she half expected him to make some move toward her bedroom. He did nothing of the kind, however, merely dropped a chaste kiss in the direction of her forehead and said good night.

The following day in the office, it was back to business as usual, though Vickie was pleasantly surprised when she decided to take a swim after work and found Benji and Susan still playing in the small wading pool. She had a chatty little conversation with Benji about his pony. Susan, though reserved at first, warmed up enough to show Vickie the kachina doll, already a prized possession. The encounter proved valuable in an unexpected way when Vickie caught, amid Susan's busy chatter, something about showing the doll to Aunt Nancy.

Nancy was the other half of the twin set. Where did she live? Nearby? Was this the hoped-for opportunity for Kathy and her hired helper to grab the kids? Vickie pried enough to learn from Benji that the visit to Aunt Nancy involved going by airplane, but at four years old, he was vague about where the big house Aunt Nancy lived in was located.

On Saturday morning, Vickie went to the office as usual. She knew she was expected to work on a weekend only if there were some emergency, but she wanted to do a bit of reorganization of the filing system. She might be here for an underhanded reason, but at least she could do her paid job to the best of her ability. Barr peered into the office at about ten o'clock and found her surrounded by a clutter of manila folders.

"What do I have to do to get you to take a little time off?" he asked, his exasperation only partly pretended. "Haul you off to Albuquerque again?"

His mention of Albuquerque gave her an odd little fluttery feeling. The day glimmered softly in her mind, a small treasure to put away and remember. "If I could borrow a horse, I thought I might take a ride this afternoon," she said briskly, shooing the warm memory of Albuquerque out of her mind. It had been years since Vickie had ridden a girl friend's gelding back in Amarillo, but she wanted to give horseback riding a try while she was here.

"I'm just on my way to check on one of the stock-watering tanks. It's out by what's left of the original old homestead house. Would you like to ride out with me and see the old place? You seemed interested in Hale Wardlow's history of the valley."

Vickie accepted the offer immediately. She changed to jeans and a plaid cotton shirt, but she had to wear sneakers because she didn't own a pair of cowboy boots. When she walked out to the corral, Barr's quick glance at the snug fit of the designer jeans around the neat curve of her derriere was approving, but he shook his head at the sneakers.

"Your ankles will be raw before we're halfway there. Wait here a minute and I'll see what I can find."

He went in the house and returned a few minutes later with a pair of multistitched boots with slim, elegant tops. The boots fit Vickie's feet almost perfectly.

"They're beautiful boots." Vickie ran her fingers over the rich leather. "But surely they're too large to be your mother's."

"They're Lou Ann's. She left them one time when she was over here." Barr's voice was innocently neutral when he added, "You don't mind, do you?"

There was a certain less innocent gleam in his sage-colored eyes that told Vickie he knew exactly how she felt about wearing the other girl's boots, but she refused to give him the satisfaction of knowing he was right. If she'd known the boots belonged to the leggy blonde, she'd never have put them on her feet! What was Lou Ann doing leaving her boots here, anyway? And from where had Barr retrieved them so quickly? His bedroom? She stomped around in the boots with more force than necessary while Barr led two saddled horses out of the corral. He expertly adjusted the stirrup leathers to fit Vickie's legs.

They rode west toward the juniper-covered foothills, circling the edge of a green field, which had an extensive sprinkler irrigation system mounted on wheels. Barr casually gave her a bit of family history, telling her how the Chandlers had hung on when others in the valley gave up and how, later, they had increased and consolidated their holdings and turned to modern, large-scale ranching methods with deep wells for irrigation.

"So now you have it all efficiently organized. You raise the cattle here, and Niles fattens them for market on the feed lot in Arizona," Vickie commented.

Barr laughed. "We go one step further. My sister Nancy and her husband own the best steak house in Phoenix, and we supply the beef, of course."

Nancy lived in Phoenix. And the kids were going to visit her sometime soon. Another cord of the net tightened into place. But instead of feeling pleased with her amateur spy work, Vickie felt a sudden surge of self-dislike. Here, in the fresh open air, with sunshine on her hair, the good feel of the horse beneath her and

Barr laughing beside her, her underhanded purpose on the ranch suddenly seemed untenable.

And yet what Ric had done to Kathy wasn't right either. . . .

Barr saw the quick shadow cross her face. "Something wrong?" he questioned lightly.

Avoiding an answer, Vickie kicked the willing gelding into a lope. Then, gaining confidence, she urged him into a full gallop. Her hair streamed like a dark banner behind her, and she felt a wonderful, exultant sense of freedom as the horse took a flying leap over a small gully. Just for today, she thought recklessly, she would put aside her ulterior motive here and enjoy the sunshine and pounding hoofs and Barr's laughter floating behind her. She leaned low over the horse's neck, urging him on, and together they raced with the wind.

When she finally reined the horse to a walk, her hair tumbled into a disheveled cloud around her flushed face, and the soreness of her inner thighs reminded her of just how long it had been since she had ridden a horse.

"I was under the impression you didn't know how to ride," Barr observed. He had stayed right with her on the wild dash along the dusty road. "I think I was wrong."

"Maybe it's something you never forget. I rode a lot when I was a girl back in Am—" Vickie caught herself before the incriminating word was out. She must never say anything to give any of the Chandlers even the slightest hint that would connect her with the city where Kathy lived. "Back in California," she finished lamely. It was an unhappy reminder that she couldn't let her guard down even on such a glorious day as this.

They rode along side by side at a more sedate pace. Vickie had the uneasy feeling that Barr wanted to ask some questions about her past, but she kept him busy with her own questions about the ranch and the area. He checked the stock tank, supplied with water by a windmill, and found everything in good order. They wandered through what remained of the old homestead.

Some small, tumble-down logs and rough boards, once painstakingly hauled from the mountains, were all that was left, but Vickie noted a leaning shelf by a window, and her imagination supplied an image of some staunch Chandler woman of long ago hopefully adding a feminine touch with a few wildflowers in a glass jar. The wind sighed through the open cracks and windows without glass, stirring a hint of dry old dust and long-gone memories. Vickie could understand why many had given up and gone away. The hardships in this harsh, lonely land must have been many. But the Chandlers had stubbornly stayed and defiantly prospered.

"I feel—regretful about this," Barr murmured as he eyed the mournful remnants. An old metal washtub rang with a sad clang when he kicked it. "I feel we should have done more to preserve the heritage of our family's past. Maybe you have to reach a certain age before you start thinking about connecting past and future generations."

Vickie gave him a thoughtful glance. *Connecting past and future generations.* Was he thinking of children of his own? Why had he never married?

A barbed-wire fence of fairly recent origin protected the old homestead from cattle, but it was obvious that the fence had come too late to preserve much of the past. Vickie wasn't sure anything more would have helped, anyway. Time and nature took their toll. *Time.* The amount of time during which she would be a part of all this suddenly seemed painfully brief, like a life cut short too soon.

Barr was quiet as they rode away from the crumbling building, though she knew his subdued mood was for a far different reason than her own. His retreat was brief, however. "Hungry?" he inquired.

"Starved," Vickie admitted. She threw off her own dispirited feeling. "But this appears to be one place the hamburger and taco stands haven't reached."

"Ah, but you're reckoning without Chandler foresight and ingenuity." Barr grinned and led the way to the gentle rise of the first low foothill and dismounted beside a patch of juniper. "While you were changing clothes, Doñela packed a few sandwiches for us. And I brought a blanket for m'lady to sit on." He untied the blanket from behind his saddle and spread it with a flourish in the sparse shade.

What she really needed, Vickie thought with a groan as she slid off the horse, was a *pillow*. She doubted if she'd be able to walk tomorrow. And Lou Ann's expensive boots were rubbing a raw spot on her heel. No doubt Lou Ann's revenge for Vickie's being out here with Barr, Vickie thought wryly. What was their relationship, anyway?

"Just drop the reins," Barr called. "The horses are trained to stand ground-tied."

Vickie slipped off the offending boots and ate sitting cross-legged. Barr tried the position but couldn't quite manage it with his long legs.

"A position meant only for the weaker sex, anyway," he muttered.

"Spoken like a true male chauvinist," Vickie retorted.

Barr just grinned. The ham and cheese sandwiches were delicious and satisfying, and Barr even produced a thermos of coffee from the saddlebags. He lay back on the blanket when he had finished eating, head pillowed on his hands.

"How come you happened to ride all the way out here?" Vickie asked idly as she munched on one of Doñela's good oatmeal cookies. She knew that the horse was still indispensable for certain cattle work, but more often a truck or pickup was used to get around the big ranch. The dusty two-track road on which they had ridden had obviously been traversed by vehicle many times. Even from this distance, the ranch buildings were clearly visible on the flat valley floor.

"You said you wanted a horseback ride. I figured you'd turn me down if all I offered was a bumpy pickup ride out here," Barr said candidly.

Vickie glanced at him over her shoulder, uncertain whether to take him seriously. And even less certain what to make of him if he were telling the truth. "Are you always so considerate of a new secretary's wishes?" she parried lightly.

"Not always. Frankly, I was scared to death of the husband hunter."

The small noise of skepticism Vickie made was not entirely ladylike. "I doubt that. I'd say you're probably quite adept at evading eager female clutches." Vickie paused and amended that with a certain tartness. "At least those clutches which have permanence in mind."

"You make me sound like the Playboy of the Golden West."

Vickie didn't have that opinion of him exactly. It was obvious he put too much into the ranch to attain playboy status. But she couldn't help being curious. "So why haven't you ever married?"

He rolled over on his side, facing her. The curve of his mouth told her he was planning to give her some lighthearted explanation, but unexpectedly he changed his mind. "I don't know. I've come close a few times." His muscled shoulders moved in a small shrug. "I guess I just never met a woman I loved so much I couldn't live without her. And I figured it wasn't worth getting tied up in a marriage for any less important reason."

"So you just go around breaking hearts and giving the valley a bad name, according to Lou Ann."

Vickie had intended the remark to be lightly teasing to alleviate the sudden seriousness between them, but his retort had a searing intensity.

"I doubt that I ever left any woman as afraid of men in general as you are."

Vickie's breath caught in her throat. His eyes held no hint of the laughter that often danced there.

"What—what makes you think I'm afraid of men?" She tried to sound lightly scoffing, but the words came out tremulous.

"This."

He reached out and caught her by the wrist, pulling her down beside him. Instinctively, she resisted, squirming and rolling and twisting sideways until they were both tangled in the blanket. She got her knees between them, but he threw a long leg over the bent knees and held her immobilized with his greater strength. In furious frustration, she pummeled his chest with her fists, her fury only increasing as his broad chest absorbed the blows as if they were no more than love taps. She slammed the heel of her hand into his chin. That blow brought a grunt of reaction but not release. He captured her wrist in his powerful hand and wedged her other hand between their bodies.

By that time, Vickie was panting, and her tumbled hair was in her eyes, and she was powerless to do anything but glare at him.

"You see?" he said softly. "The minute a man touches you, you go all tense and then turn into a wildcat."

"Of course I fight," Vickie snapped, "if I'm grabbed and thrown around like a—a sack of beans."

56

He hadn't really been that rough. He'd used a velvet strength more than rough force to subdue her, but she had to say something insulting to keep him from touching her again. Why *did* she overreact whenever he touched her? she wondered wildly. Not for the reason he thought, that it was some aftereffect of her "bad marriage." But she was at a loss to understand the reaction herself. She had certainly been touched before, even enjoyed a few passionate kisses, though she had never felt in any danger of being swept away by passion. But there was something different about contact with Barr, like the ends of two charged wires arcing to meet each other with an explosive spark.

"Are you telling me it's my approach that's all wrong, then?" The familiar teasing gleam was back in his eyes, but his voice had a certain huskiness that told her he wasn't entirely teasing.

Another protectively tart retort rose to Vickie's lips, but she had no opportunity to get it out. He tilted his head and covered her mouth softly with his own. She pulled her head back, but his mouth followed her, tenderly relentless, until her hair touched the blanket and she could retreat no farther.

The kiss was an assault and an exploration, but an assault so sweet and an exploration so tender that Vickie felt as if her veins flowed with warm honey. His tongue searched her mouth, testing, questioning, but with no trace of uncertainty. Her taut neck muscles yielded to the gently insistent pressure, until she could hold her head stiffly rigid no longer. She heard his small rumble of satisfaction as she yielded and the muscles went slack, and his mouth plundered hers in conquering possession.

But she would yield no further, she vowed silently. Her tongue met his in intimate duel as she resisted him, waging a silent battle of lips and tongue and male-female wills. And even as she thought she was holding her own in the small fierce battle, she felt a new and even more dangerous assault as his finger tips crept between the buttons of her blouse and found the rounded curve of her breast. Treacherously, beyond her control, the breast seemed to swell, straining as if it possessed a will of its own to snuggle into his cupped hand. She fought that battle with all her concentration, pushing his hand away with her own, only to find that his lips had found yet another vulnerable place in the curve of her throat.

"Please . . ." she murmured helplessly, hardly knowing what she asked. She felt her defenses crumbling, attacked by demanding forces from within that battled to meet the sweet fire of Barr's assault from outside.

"Vickie, Vickie, what did he do to you? How did he hurt you?" Barr murmured gently against the damp sheen of her throat. "You mustn't close yourself away from love because of something one man did to you."

In the cloud of unfamiliar desire fogging her mind, his words bewildered her for a moment. And then she remembered. Her "bad marriage." At the moment, the thought rose like an island of rescue in a dangerous sea, and she desperately leaped for it. "It was just a—a very bad marriage, and he said things—and did things—and once you've been hurt—I mean, it just left me with the feeling that I never wanted to get involved again." She stumbled awkwardly through the explanation, her words broken not because of something that had happened in the past but what was happening now.

"Never is a long time," he said softly. "Once you've been married and known a man's love, even if things went wrong in the end—"

His body slid over hers with a small, intimately

suggestive movement, and Vickie fought an urge to wrap her legs around his. Instead, she struggled again, twisting her shoulders and head and trying to get her hands between her breasts and his chest. In response, he simply let the full weight of his body crush her against the blanket until she couldn't move. Then, as carefully as if her hands held wildcat claws, he grasped a wrist in each hand and spread her arms out at full length. Vickie felt a button on her blouse give way under the strain.

"I take it you think any divorcée is fair game?" she snapped. "Any previously married woman must surely be starved for sex, and you're ready and willing to supply it?" Anger made it easier to ignore the warm ripples of desire that pulsed through her, and she was almost grateful that he had made the outrageous remark.

"In the—heat of the moment, perhaps I didn't phrase that too well," Barr murmured ruefully.

His mouth curved in that good-humored twist to which Vickie knew she was almost as vulnerable as she was to his passionate kisses and caresses. Oh, damn, damn, she groaned inwardly.

"I only meant—" He raised up, cautiously releasing her hands. "Would you tell me about your marriage and what went wrong before I say or do anything more to hurt or upset you?"

Vickie scooted to a sitting position and tried wildly to think of something. What went wrong with marriages? Money? In-laws? Sex? Her blouse was gaping open where the button had popped off, and her bra felt as if it had suddenly become too small for her. She clutched nervously at the blouse.

"Well, it's a—a rather personal and painful subject. . . ."

He sat up beside her, his firmly muscled thigh touching her crossed legs. "Vickie, haven't you ever heard that when you get thrown from a horse, the only thing to do is get on and ride again?"

"Getting thrown from a marriage is a little different than getting thrown from a horse!" She swallowed. "Honestly, Barr, I'd rather not talk about it." And that, she thought weakly to herself, was the honest-to-God truth for a change. "Shouldn't we start back?"

"I suppose."

Barr replaced the cup on the thermos, and Vickie gathered up the plastic wrappers that were all that remained of their lunch. Her body was beginning to feel stiff all over from the ride, and Barr noted the jerky movement.

"Sit down in front of me," he commanded. "I'll rub some of the soreness out of your back and shoulders."

Vickie hesitated warily, and he held up empty hands as if to protest his innocence of some unspoken accusation.

"I know what I'm doing. Honestly. I became an expert at massage when my younger brothers were involved in high school athletics."

She sat between his outstretched legs, and he gave her a thorough and expert massage, starting at her neck and working across the top ridges of her shoulders and down her back. He rubbed and kneaded and chopped lightly, grumbling once that he could do a better job if her blouse and bra straps weren't in the way.

"Just work around them and do the best you can," she advised sweetly. Without thinking about it, she rested her hands lightly on his long legs curved around her. Her back and shoulders did feel marvelously relaxed by the time he finished, and she told him so. She started to scoot away and then winced. "But I'm afraid that isn't where I'm going to be most sore in the morning."

"Right. You're going to be sore right—there." His hand curved around her inner thigh, closing lightly over the sore skin and muscles, then moving slightly to pinpoint a particularly sensitive area over the bone. His other hand slid around her to touch the opposite thigh. But now the touch was feathery caress, no more the hearty athletic massage. The warmth of his touch seeped through the denim, and then his finger tips whispered a pathway across the even more intimate parts of her body as they drifted up to the bare skin beneath her blouse.

The sound she meant as protest came out instead as a small soft moan of mingled pleasure and desire as his hands cupped her breasts. She leaned back against him, head on his shoulder. His mouth softly nuzzled the side of her neck, and her tousled hair fell across his face.

"Your hair was made for a man to touch," he whispered, turning his head to let the soft dark cloud caress his cheek.

In response, she reached up and tangled her fingers in his hair. It felt as it looked, streaked with warm sunlight, crisp yet softly curling against his neck and around her fingers.

She was never conscious of his hands moving around to unfasten her bra, but her breasts spilled free. He caught the naked, rounded flesh in his hands, cupping it.

"Your skin was made to caress. . . ." His hands explored the silken treasure, and his touch curled long tendrils of fire ever deeper into her body. "And your mouth was born to kiss. . . ."

His body shifted to turn her half around to face him as his mouth sought hers. The kiss was deep, and still his hands cupped her breasts with a gentle pressure. She felt as if she were caught in a triangle of fiery pleasure with his hands on her breasts and his mouth locked to hers, and she was surrounded with the warmth of his chest against her back and his legs curved around her thighs. She was melting, boneless, liquid with the desire. Just when she had thought the danger was over, it was here again, more powerful than before. And the greatest danger of all was that she no longer wanted to fight it. Her finger tips trailed the smooth hard line of his jaw, and when he lifted his mouth, he caught the finger tips in his teeth and played a flickering caress on them with his tongue.

He pushed her gently down on the blanket. Her hair spread in a pool of darkness around her face, and he ran his fingers through the glowing strands. His finger tips trailed across her neck and gently unfastened the remaining buttons of her blouse. She was helpless to move anything but her eyes, which followed his.

He spread the plaid material wide and curved his palms around her breasts, the thumbs lightly caressing the already straining tips to new peaks of yearning.

"A body meant to share a man's love. . . ." His mouth dipped to the eager peaks of her breasts, and his hand stroked her with long, flowing caresses that lingered on intimate hollows and curves just long enough to make her wild for more. "And now my fighting wildcat shows that deep down inside she's truly a purring kitten."

His hand rested on the waistband of her jeans, and the small popping sound of the snap opening hit her ears like the crack of a rifle shot. The meaning and danger of what was happening finally got through to her, and she frantically scrambled away from him as if she had just come out of a trance.

She floundered across the blanket, fumbled with the

buttons of her blouse, gave it up as useless and grabbed her boots.

"Vickie!"

She slammed her feet into the boots, ran for the startled horse and moments later streaked toward the ranch house at full gallop.

Chapter Four

With one hand on the reins and the other frantically clutching the open, flapping blouse, Vickie urged her horse across the treeless valley, her thoughts as tumultuous as the storm of physical arousal Barr had caused within her.

What had come over her to let the physical contact between them go so far? She had not only *let* the kisses and caresses go that far, she had *wanted* them. And more! Why? She had never thought of herself as having a particularly passionate nature, had, in fact, wondered occasionally if her physical desires were not somewhat below normal levels.

She wondered that no more. Now she knew she had simply never before encountered the man who could penetrate the barrier of her reserve, who could turn her blood into wildfire. She wished with all her heart that she had not encountered him now, because she could not, *must* not, get involved physically or emotionally with Barr Chandler! There could be no happy future for such involvement, no future at all except heartbreak. She had come here for a specific purpose, and when her mission was accomplished, she must run, knowing full well that Barr would despise her for the loss she had helped inflict on his family.

Even if she decided to throw caution to the winds and follow the desires of her body, accepting the fact that she and Barr could never have more than a temporary affair, there was one small complication. If they ever made love, Barr was far too sophisticated not to recognize immediately that her story of a previous marriage was a complete fabrication. She was, in the affectionately teasing words of her more experienced Shreveport roommate, "quaintly virginal," and that fact would never escape Barr's attention. And once a single thread gave way in the web of lies she had constructed around herself, Vickie knew the whole fragile structure could collapse. The end result would be the same: Barr would despise her. And there would be the added despair of failure in her mission here. She would not even have the satisfaction of knowing she had aided the family *she* loved.

No, she must not give in to the wild desires Barr had aroused in her; she must close the cracks he had already opened in her defenses. She could hear Barr now, the roar of his voice faintly audible even above the thunder of the horse's pounding hoofs. She did not slacken the animal's racing flight; instead, she leaned lower into the tangled banner of his mane to urge him on.

Barr was furious, she thought with a certain grim satisfaction. That would make her task easier. Resisting his fury would be far less difficult than resisting the heart-tugging grin or the seductive caresses of his mouth and hands.

Out of the corner of her eye, she saw his stallion inching up on her, the flaring nostrils edging past her own gelding's flank and drawing even with her stirrup.

"What the hell are you doing?" Barr yelled. "Stop your horse!"

"No!"

With the same ruthless swiftness with which he had

captured the man who tried to steal her purse, he reached down and grabbed the reins beneath her horse's jaw. Vickie slashed at his arm with the free end of the reins, but in doing so, she had to let go of her blouse, and the shirt tails immediately flapped in her face. When Barr brought both horses to a snorting standstill, blouse and unfastened bra were wound around Vickie's chest and throat and arms in a tangled disarray that exposed more than it concealed.

"You're planning to race into the ranch yard like that?" Barr snapped. His insolent gaze raked the naked breasts thrusting through the maze of fabric.

"Let go of my horse!" she raged. When he didn't comply, she abandoned the reins in frustration and struggled frantically to cover her breasts and disentangle herself from the labyrinth of straps, sleeves and shirt tails. Barr just sat on his horse and watched, making no attempt to conceal the fact that he *was* watching.

"You might have the decency to look the other way!" Tears of frustration gathered in Vickie's eyes until finally Barr wrapped both sets of reins around his saddle horn.

"Let me," he said laconically.

Vickie glared at him for a moment, but she obviously wasn't making much progress on her own. With deft hands, he reached over and untangled the hook on the bra from the fabric of the blouse. It was evidently the key to unraveling the tangle, and she glared at him again as she snatched the front of the blouse closed.

"Lean forward," he commanded. When she didn't obey, he tugged meaningfully on the still unfastened bra. Reluctantly, she leaned forward, letting her breasts fall naturally into the lacy cups of the bra. He fastened the hook and straightened the back of her blouse.

66

"Thank you," she said with stiff politeness as she buttoned the blouse, but inwardly she was still raging. A lot she had to be thankful to him for! It was he who had originally undone all those buttons and hooks. And one button was missing, thanks to him. With one hand, she determinedly held the gap shut. "May I please have the reins now?"

"If you think you can ride on back to the ranch at a decent pace. The horse is winded."

Guiltily, Vickie realized that was true. The gelding wasn't as young as Barr's muscled stallion. She gave the horse an apologetic pat on the neck. She also managed to collect a few scraps of her scattered composure. There was an odd expression on Barr's face. Anger still darkened his gray-green eyes, like sage under the shadow of storm clouds, but something else hovered around his mouth. Defiantly, she encouraged the anger.

"You should have warned me when you hired me that you expected skills beyond simple typing and bookkeeping!"

The taunt had the desired effect. White grooves outlined the corners of his mouth. He flung the reins to her and whirled his horse toward the ranch house without a backward glance in her direction. Her gelding automatically followed the stallion's lead. They rode silently past the green field with the fresh, damp scent of irrigated alfalfa. Beyond the field, she saw something she had missed before, the blue gleam of a small metal hangar with a plane anchored outside and wind socks blowing along the landing strip.

But awareness of all that was somewhere on the edge of her consciousness. Inwardly, she seethed, berating herself for her foolishness in coming along on this ride, cursing the desires of a body that had always seemed so trustworthy and obedient before encountering Barr, but which now seemed to possess a treacherous will of its own. Barr himself did not escape her fury, of course. The nerve of him, the arrogance!

At the gate to the corral, he dismounted. Vickie slid off the gelding, her legs feeling permanently bowed.

"You're going to be stiff and sore," Barr observed dispassionately. "Better go take a long, hot soak in the tub."

"I'll brush the horse down first. He's all sweaty."

"I'll have one of the men do it."

Vickie nodded and handed the reins to him, then turned to leave. He caught her elbow with one hand.

"Vickie . . ." There was a dark chase of expressions on his face, fleeting bits of anger and exasperation mingled with something softer.

"Yes?" She kept an aloof, distant look on her face in spite of the sudden somersault of her heart. She had the wild feeling that he might shake her. Or kiss her. And that he wasn't sure himself which he was going to do.

"I'm sorry about today. No matter what you think, I didn't have anything devious in mind when we rode out there." The circle of his grip made a warm band around her arm. "I know you went through a rough time in your marriage, and I'm not—unsympathetic."

"You have a strange way of showing sympathy!"

His mouth twisted in a small, rueful smile. "I suppose so. When I'm holding you, other feelings tend to crowd out my sympathy and understanding. But you didn't have to race away as if the devil himself were after you."

"I'm not certain the devil himself *wasn't* after me!" she retorted tartly.

"A clear, simple *no* would have been sufficient," he suggested wryly. "I'm not such an insensitive clod that I can't take 'no' for an answer."

Vickie caught her full lower lip between her teeth.

She had been prepared for his fury and contempt. She had worked up a righteous anger and scorn of her own. But she was not prepared for his understanding or this mixture of rueful amusement and wry regret. At the moment, he was being so damned infuriatingly *nice*.

"I suppose I just need time to—to recover," she stammered, keeping up the protective pretense of an earlier unhappy marriage.

He tilted his head thoughtfully. "I can be patient." He ran his hand up her arm and throat and combed his fingers through the dark, wind-blown tangle of her hair. Finally, his hand settled beneath her chin, cupping it lightly. "Within limits," he added softly.

Then he flashed her a rakish smile and led the horses into the corral, leaving Vickie weakly uncertain if he was warning, promising or just teasing her. He could be maddening, first in one way and then another.

She did, however, follow his advice and took a long, hot bath, adding her own private medicine of scented, bubbling bath oil, followed by a rubdown with a soothing lotion.

By the next day, soreness still twinged her thighs and derriere, but her legs no longer felt permanently bent out of shape. She slept luxuriously late, skipped breakfast and took a refreshing dip in the pool. Several house guests had arrived the previous evening in the casual come-and-go that characterized life on the ranch. About two o'clock, everyone gathered in the dining room for the sit-down Sunday family dinner that Mrs. Chandler insisted upon.

Mrs. Chandler sat at one end of the table, Barr at the other. Vickie unexpectedly but delightedly found herself next to Benji and Susan. Across the table was a middle-aged woman, whose name had escaped Vickie, who seemed positively enchanted with the children. She asked them about themselves and their ponies, how old they were and half a dozen other questions. Vickie felt so proud of the kids. They were so adorable, polite yet brightly talkative with the woman. Susan held up a shy three fingers when asked her age. Then Benji was telling the woman all about a bird he and his grandma had rescued the day before. It had flown into the picture window and been temporarily stunned but had recovered and flown away.

"Sometimes they don't fly away," Benji added. "Then they go to heaven. That's where my mommy is, you know."

The woman looked startled. "What did you say?"

"I said sometimes the birds go to be with my mommy in heaven," Benji reiterated in his clear, childish bell tones.

Vickie choked on the mouthful of roast chicken she had started to swallow. She gasped and reached for a glass of water. The woman evidently decided this mother-in-heaven subject should not be pursued and retreated to a safer conversation about ponies. Vickie could only sit there shaking with anger and frustration, all appetite gone.

Benji and Susan had been told their mother was *dead!* The unfairness of it, the gross injustice, infuriated Vickie. She glanced down the table where Ric was unconcernedly stuffing chicken into his mouth, and she felt a sudden blind hatred for him. Her angry gaze settled on Barr at the end of the table, laughing and handsome and carefree, and she hated him as well. And Mrs. Chandler, also, elegant in her froth of silver-embroidered lace. All of them were in on it, a conspiracy to deny that the children's mother even existed. And Vickie could do nothing about it. Nothing! She couldn't tell Susan and Benji that it was all a pack of lies, that their mother was alive and that she loved and wanted them very much. She was helpless to

70

do anything but let the children go on believing that their mother was dead and in heaven.

It was all Vickie could do to sit there quietly while the dessert was served. She savagely stabbed her chocolate soufflé to bits and then shoved the pieces around until eventually, mercifully, the endless meal was over. She scraped her chair back and hurriedly excused herself, knowing she had to get to the privacy of her own room before she exploded in fury and recklessly exposed everything.

She didn't even notice the arm shoot out to check her hasty flight until she collided with it. "Several of us thought we'd run into Albuquerque and take in a jazz combo that's playing at one of the lounges," Barr said. "Would you like to come along?"

"No." Vickie snapped the blunt rejection with no attempt at courtesy. She shot him a darkly angry look, detoured around his arm and moved on toward the hallway.

In her room, she turned the lock on the knob and leaned her back against the door. How could they have told those innocent children that their mother was dead? It was cruel—unthinkable! For a short while, Vickie's attitude toward the Chandlers had softened. Sometimes she had wondered uneasily if what she was doing was *right*. Now she had no more doubts. She would get those children out of here and back to Kathy if she had to steal them herself!

She jumped as a knock vibrated against her back.

"Vickie? Are you in there? Are you all right?" Barr's low tones held concern.

Vickie rubbed a hand across her eyes, surprised to find they were wet with tears. She blinked and cleared her throat. "I'm fine."

"Is something wrong?" he persisted.

"I'm just—tired," she evaded.

"Let me in."

"No!" She could see her reflection in the mirror, eyes incriminatingly red-rimmed around the edges and unnaturally bright with tears. Damn, damn, damn, she muttered angrily to herself. Why was she crying when what she really wanted to do was smash some precious Chandler possession? And she mustn't do either, she reminded herself, not if she wanted to succeed in the purpose for which she had come here. "Please go away. I'm going to lie down for a while." She kept her voice as distant as the far side of the moon.

"Vickie, I want to know what's wrong. Let me in."

His words were followed by a small, warning creak of the hinges, as if he were lightly testing his weight against their resistance. He wouldn't break down the door—would he? Surely not for such a minor matter as this, surely not with a houseful of guests milling around! Yet suddenly she wasn't sure. Barr had that unpredictable streak, and he could be both ruthless and reckless when challenged.

She hesitated a moment more, then said angrily, "Very well. Just a moment." She dabbed her eyes and nose with a tissue, then unlocked and opened the door.

He stepped inside, glanced around as if half expecting to find a strange man lurking inside and quickly closed the door behind him. "You're crying," he accused.

"No, not really," she denied in spite of the unmistakable evidence.

"Vickie, what *is* wrong?" He sounded honestly perplexed. "You're not still upset about yesterday?"

"No, of course not." Vickie made a gesture dismissing that possibility, deliberately downgrading its importance even though each thought of those intoxicating moments made her feel a bit feverish and giddy. On second thought, she suddenly wished she had let him think it *was* yesterday that had upset her as he abruptly zeroed in on the truth. Or at least a portion of the truth.

"You were fine when you came to dinner. I was watching you." His eyes narrowed speculatively. "I also saw your reaction when Benji made his little speech about the birds and his mother being in heaven. That was when you started to get upset, wasn't it?"

"Perhaps," she returned evasively. She rubbed her palms, nervously damp, with the already shredded tissue. She made a small production out of tossing the tissue in the wastepaper basket, then took a comb and fussed with her hair in front of the mirror. Her evasive tactics did not work.

"Why?" Barr demanded bluntly. "I know you're a—" He hesitated momentarily, and then his voice softened slightly as he added "—a sensitive person, but I don't see why you should be so upset by what Benji said. He wasn't upset."

The tears spurted back to Vickie's eyes. No, Benji wasn't upset. He was so clear-eyed and sweet and trusting. And it wasn't fair! Not to the kids or to Kathy.

"I guess I—I just hadn't realized until then that the children's mother was dead," she said lamely. "It suddenly seemed so sad."

A ridge of hard muscle jerked to prominence along Barr's angular jaw line. He walked to the window and stood scowling at the pool. He turned and looked at Vickie for a long, calculating moment, as if trying to decide something.

"Their mother isn't dead," he finally said abruptly.

"She isn't?" Vickie's astonishment at the statement was as real as if the information were actually a surprise. The surprise, of course, was that he had chosen to tell her the truth.

"Ric had told the children their mother was dead and

in heaven before he ever brought them here. I don't know why. I didn't approve, but I didn't feel I could openly contradict what their father had told them." Barr was scowling, angry, though Vickie was uncertain at the moment if the anger was directed at Ric for originating the lie or at her for digging it out.

She turned back to the dressing table, eyeing his reflection in a section of the triple mirror as she absent-mindedly made a pretense of doing something more with her hair.

"How does your mother feel about this deception?"

Barr's broad shoulders moved in an impatient shrug. "She doesn't approve, either, but again, it's a touchy situation. Ric doesn't have the hair-trigger temper he used to have. He's grown up a lot. I think he's happy being in charge of all the equipment and mechanical work here on the ranch. He sold cars back East for a while and hated that. But still, there's always the possibility that he could become angry and just pick up the kids and leave. We wouldn't want that to happen. Benji and Susan are very—" He hesitated before adding in an odd tone, "Very precious to us."

Precious. It was an unexpected word, one that seemed out of character for Barr. He used it reluctantly, as if he would have preferred something less sentimental but could find no other word that quite fit the situation.

And suddenly Vickie realized just how accurate the word was. By now she had heard enough family gossip to know that Niles and his wife, Serena, despite persistent effort, had no children. Medical problems had forced Nancy into surgery that meant she could never bear children. Barr, of course, had remained aloof from the whole marriage-parenthood situation. So there were only Ric's children in the family, little Benji and Susan.

But they were just as precious to Kathy and Aunt Verla, Vickie thought helplessly to herself, wanting to cry it out. Instead, she said cautiously, "What about the children's mother?"

"She lives over in Texas. I met her a few times. I'm afraid she found the Chandler clan somewhat overwhelming. She seemed nice enough, kind of sweet, actually, but rather immature."

Probably an accurate enough description of Kathy, Vickie thought grudgingly, at least as far as it went. But it left out more than it included. It said nothing about how crazy in love Kathy was with Ric when they married, nor did it note that the loss of her children had matured her with cruel efficiency. "How does Ric feel about her?" Vickie asked.

"I really don't know. He doesn't say much. He was very much in love at first, but . . ." Barr's voice trailed off, and he shrugged.

Suppose she told Barr everything, Vickie thought with a sudden wild impulse. He cared deeply about the children; that she knew. He stood by the window, with sunlight, reflected from the pool, dancing across the carved mask of his rugged, sun-darkened features. He looked what he was, powerful both in physical strength and as head of the Chandler clan, but Vickie sensed a certain frustration in him about this situation over which he lacked total control. He disapproved of telling the children that Kathy was dead. Perhaps together she and Barr could help Kathy and Ric work out something that would be more fair than the present situation. Vickie was on the verge of spilling everything when Barr spoke again.

"I'm sure Ric's wife would like to get hold of the kids, but we have a very good lawyer protecting Ric and the children's interests, of course."

This time his voice held a certain confidence that

75

suddenly infuriated Vickie. Yes, indeed, they undoubtedly had an excellent lawyer, she thought bitterly, the best money could buy. No wonder Kathy was afraid to go into court and confront their power and money!

"Are you really certain that Ric's interests and the children's interests are one and the same?" Vickie demanded recklessly. She instantly regretted the defiant words, but even more, she regretted the softening that had almost led her to make a disastrous mistake. She must be on guard every minute against both Barr's strength and her own weakness.

"What do you mean by that?" Barr walked over and stood behind her, his eyes meeting hers in the mirror.

"Nothing." She raked the comb savagely through her hair.

He took the comb from her and gently slid it through her hair, pulling the dark glowing strands away from her face. The mirror showed a pink-gold luminosity to her skin, partly a result of yesterday's ride in the sun, partly a blood-surging reaction from within to the touch of his hands. The comb continued to glide through her hair, a strangely sensual caress, almost hypnotic. It seemed to pull her back against the lean length of his body.

She jerked away before she was completely captured and lost under the spell. "Don't you think the children need their mother? Doesn't she have some rights?"

"She didn't seem too concerned about *Ric's* rights when several times she wouldn't even let him see Susan and Benji."

"I don't believe that!" She would never have done that! But a certain wariness leaped into Barr's eyes, and Vickie made a panicky retreat. "I—I mean, it just seems so unlikely. Surely one parent wouldn't deny the other. . . ."

Barr tossed the comb on the dressing table. "Unfortunately, parents sometimes use their children to fight their battles. It's a no-win situation."

True enough, Vickie thought unhappily. But in this case, one parent had all the advantages in the battle because Barr Chandler was on his side. Couldn't Barr see that Ric was lying, just as he had lied to the children about Kathy's being in heaven? Was Barr's fierce family loyalty so blind that he could accept this injustice?

Yes, she answered herself grimly, it was.

"I take it this protectiveness about Ric's wife's 'rights' has something to do with your own unhappy marriage?"

Barr sounded as if he were using his considerable self-control to rein in an exasperation with her attitude, making a determined effort to be understanding. At the moment, the effort was wasted on Vickie, but she confirmed his explanation rather than take a chance on his discovering the real reason for her agitation.

"Yes, I suppose so," she said stiffly. "I do tend to see the woman's point of view."

"But you mustn't let one bad experience sour you on all men for life," he said softly. He took her hand and led her back to the mirror. He put his arms around her from behind and leaned his head against her temple. "Look at you. You're all upset over nothing."

Nothing! Vickie ground her teeth together, raging at her helplessness, aching to lash out and tell him exactly what she thought of him and Ric and all the Chandlers who stuck together, right or wrong.

"Your eyes are shooting green-gold sparks." He rubbed his jaw lightly against her temple as his eyes held hers in the mirror. "I could almost think you were angry with *me* again."

She couldn't let him know that his accusation was correct. But neither could she bring herself totally to deny it. "Why should I be angry with you?" she retorted evasively.

"Because I arouse something in you that you don't want aroused." He turned his head slightly, and his lips brushed her temple. "You'd prefer to stay tucked away in your safe little shell where you can't get hurt again."

He was wrong, of course. He saw everything in light of her "bad marriage." She could find a certain grim satisfaction in the knowledge that he wasn't as all-knowing as he imagined himself to be. But he was all too correct in his self-assured statement that he aroused something in her that she did not want aroused. Even now, angry as she was with him and everything Chandler, she could feel a hot tingle of awareness as his hands slid up and down her bare arms. She watched the movement in the mirror, hands that could manage a spirited stallion or collar a thief now gliding across her bare skin with sensuous tenderness. He dipped his head and nibbled at the sensitive curve between her throat and shoulder. Her skin felt incandescent under the touch, and she heard a ragged breath and realized it was her own.

"Barr . . . don't . . ."

"You have nowhere to run this time, little wildcat," he murmured. "You're already in your hiding place, and there's no escape."

Gently, he turned her in his arms, framed her face with his hands and with slow deliberation lowered his mouth to hers. The kiss was deep and lingering, sweet and fiery, not so much an exploration as a claiming of what he had explored before.

Mouth still clamped to hers, he picked her up and swung her toward the bed. She caught a glimpse of their reflection in the mirror, her full skirt flung back over a length of slim thigh, the imprint of his sun-browned hand a dark intruder against her honey-gold skin.

Barr stood beside the bed, one knee braced on the edge as he lowered her to the quilted spread. Finally, his lips parted from hers.

"I almost forgot. . . ."

"Forgot what?" Vickie whispered. She felt a strange sense of loss as his mouth left hers.

"Forgot that I'm not supposed to do this." He smoothed the tangled skirt that had crept up still farther to expose the rounded curve of her hip, but he managed to make the gesture a tantalizing caress. "I'm being patient, remember?"

He smiled at her, a wickedly amused grin that was both teasing and lightly mocking, and Vickie had the furious feeling that she'd been tricked. He'd led her on with the full intent of showing her that he could make her dizzy with desire and then let her go, that he could leave her feeling as frustratingly unfulfilled as she left him. Angrily, she realized that her arms were wound around his neck, holding him close, almost as if she were trying to pull him down to join her on the bed. Abruptly, she flung her hands aside, releasing him, and he straightened and stepped away from the bed.

"You're sure you don't want to run into Albuquerque for a while?" he asked casually, with one hand on the doorknob. His expression was unruffled, in sharp contrast to her agitated flush.

"No!"

He just smiled again before quietly closing the door behind him. Vickie was left with a variety of frustrations and angers.

She was helpless, at least temporarily, to do anything about the lie being told to the children about their mother.

She was equally helpless, it appeared, to do anything about the explosive desire Barr aroused in her, desire that he was so infuriatingly aware that he *did* arouse.

Angrily, she flung a pillow at the door, disgusted when it fell short of its mark and plopped noiselessly to the carpet, denying her even the satisfaction of a solid, retaliatory thud against the door.

Chapter Five

Vickie telephoned Kathy again that evening. Without definite information to give, she was reluctant to contact Kathy, but when the opportunity to place a phone call safely presented itself, she didn't want to let it slip by. Mrs. Chandler, murmuring something about her back bothering her, had retired early. Ric and the kids were absorbed in television in the den. Barr and the house guests hadn't yet returned from Albuquerque. Vickie doubted that they would be back until much later, but just to be safe, she left the office in darkness while she placed the collect call to Amarillo.

Kathy answered with a breathless "Yes!" when the operator's bored voice asked if she would accept a collect call from a Vickie Thornton.

Vickie hastened to tell Kathy that she still couldn't give any definite date or time when the children would be off the ranch. She wanted to give the bad news first. "But there is a definite possibility the kids are going to be taken to visit their Aunt Nancy in Phoenix before long," she added encouragingly. "That's a lot farther away, of course. . . ."

"We'll manage," Kathy returned fervently. "Just let me know when and where. Do you know who will take them or how they'll go?"

"Benji talked about going by airplane, and I think Barr has the only pilot's license. The ranch has a plane, you know. I rather imagine Mrs. Chandler will go along."

"Do you talk to the kids much?" Kathy's voice was wistful. "Do they ever mention me?"

Vickie bit her lip, wondering what to say. She couldn't shock Kathy by telling her that Benji and Susan thought she was "in heaven." But neither did she want to hurt her by saying that the children seldom mentioned her. "Benji said something about you just today," she murmured finally.

"What?" Kathy's eagerness gave Vickie's heart a painful wrench.

"Just that you—weren't here. I'm sure they miss you," she added hurriedly.

"Sometimes I'm afraid they'll have forgotten me before I ever see them again." Kathy sighed. "Kitten, you'll never know how much I appreciate your sacrifice in doing this for me. I'd be lost without you."

"I don't mind, honestly," Vickie said quickly. "It's an interesting job. I went horseback riding yesterday. Last week I went into Albuquerque to talk to the ranch's CPA and then spent all afternoon wandering through the shops in Old Town."

"You went alone?" Kathy sounded a little taken back, as if she had assumed Vickie would hate every moment she was on the ranch.

Vickie hesitated before saying casually, "No, I was with Barr Chandler." Headlights flickered against the office windows. Startled, Vickie carried the phone to the window and peered through the dark panes. She was relieved when the lights turned in at the bunk-house.

"You mean you went out with *Barr?*" Kathy sounded shocked.

"No, not really. We did see a movie when we were in Albuquerque, but you couldn't really call it going *out* together."

"Kitten, you're not falling for him, are you?" Kathy asked suspiciously.

"No, of course not," Vickie answered quickly. Too quickly? she wondered with dismay. "What in the world made you ask that?"

"I don't know. Something in the way you said his name. I'm sure, if he wanted to, Barr could turn on megavolts of charm." Her voice held a certain sour scorn. "Not that he ever bothered to turn it on me, of course."

"Of course not. You're his brother's wife," Vickie said, more sharply than she intended.

"You really think a little thing like that would stop a *Chandler?*"

"You mentioned yourself what a strong family loyalty they have." Vickie took a deep breath. "Kath, they're not *evil* people. What Ric did wasn't right, and you deserve to have the kids back, but everyone here honestly loves them, too." Then she was angry at herself. What was she doing, *defending* the Chandlers?

Kathy was instantly apologetic. "Oh, Kitten, I'm sorry I'm so grumpy and jumpy." She sighed. "It's just that I miss the kids so much. And instead of getting easier, each day without them seems longer and harder than the one before. Can you blame me for being bitter about the Chandlers?"

"No, of course not." Vickie hesitated and then went on carefully. "But you have to remember that Ric may have given his mother and Barr a slanted view of the situation. I think Barr feels that what Ric did was perhaps justified because Ric has made Barr believe that several times you prevented him from seeing the children."

There was a small gulf of silence before Kathy said reluctantly, "Actually, that's true."

Vickie dropped into Barr's swivel chair, shocked. She had been so positive that Ric was lying! "That doesn't sound like you," she said finally.

"I didn't do it without good reason, of course," Kathy answered defensively. "And it certainly didn't justify Ric's stealing the kids! He was chasing around with this *tramp,* and I just didn't want the kids around that type of woman. And I'll bet Ric didn't bother to mention *that* to his brother!"

No, he probably hadn't, Vickie agreed silently. Ric might have guessed that Barr would disapprove. For all Barr's hot-blooded masculine desires, Vickie suspected that he might have some rather old-fashioned, even strait-laced ideas on the moral climate in which children should be raised.

Yet Vickie had only Kathy's word that the woman was a "tramp." Perhaps Kathy had simply been angry because Ric was seeing another woman—*any* woman—and had struck back at him through the children. And then Ric had retaliated. But perhaps the woman *was* someone undesirable and Kathy was justified in her actions. . . . And what was Ric doing seeing *any* woman when he was still married to Kathy? Oh, the situation was all so confusing!

"Kath, how do you feel about Ric now?" Vickie asked slowly. "I mean, apart from all this mess with Benji and Susan?"

Kathy sighed. "I was so much in love with him once. But isn't there some old saying about love and hate being opposite sides of the same coin? I just don't know. Sometimes I wish . . ." Her voice faded off, and then she added, almost with a note of belligerence, "I suppose he has a whole harem of girl friends there."

Did he? Vickie honestly didn't know if Ric ever saw any women or not. Guiltily, she realized that her attention had been so riveted on Barr that she hardly noticed Ric's activities. Headlights again arced across the office wall, and this time they were definitely approaching the house.

"I have to go now," Vickie said hurriedly. "Someone is coming. I'll call again when I can."

"Thanks, Kitten. And give the kids a hug and kiss for me, will you?"

Vickie hung up the phone, tiptoed to the window and concealed herself behind the draperies to watch the cars unload. Three cars had driven into Albuquerque, but now there were only two. Barr's car was missing. What did that mean?

Barr did not enlighten her on that subject the following morning at work. He was his usual self in the office: busy, efficient and thorough. But at lunch Vickie caught a name that instantly sharpened her senses. Lou Ann Wardlow.

Lou Ann Wardlow had gone into Albuquerque with the group last night. They had evidently stopped by and picked her up on the way. Was that the reason for the absence of Barr's car when the others returned? And just when had he gotten in?

No more clues were dropped, however, and Vickie could hardly come right out and ask questions. She also didn't *care* what Barr did in his out-of-office hours, she assured herself firmly. There was an undeniable physical attraction between them, but that was all it was, and the situation here would be far less complicated if Barr transferred his amorous interest to Lou Ann Wardlow. Back to Lou Ann, Vickie added to herself, since that was evidently where it had been before she arrived. She started to return Lou Ann's boots to him, then, piqued, changed her mind and kept them in her closet. Let Lou Ann someday wonder how they came to be in *her* bedroom.

Mrs. Chandler came to the office that afternoon. She had a handful of correspondence that needed answering—personal, club and charity things. She said it could wait if Vickie was busy with ranch business, but Vickie assured her that she could take the time now. Vickie kept hoping that somewhere in the correspondence there would be mention of some off-the-ranch activity with the children, doctor's or dentist's appointments, perhaps, but there was nothing. At this point, the children's visit to Phoenix sounded like the most likely possibility for the snatch—or rescue, as Kathy preferred to put it—though it was a fuzzy possibility at best. The unhappy thought had occurred to Vickie that given a four-year-old's vague sense of time and place, the visit could be scheduled for as far off as Thanksgiving or Christmas.

The only concrete information Vickie acquired about advance plans was that the house would be practically empty during the coming weekend. Mrs. Chandler was driving down to Ruidoso with some friends to watch Amanda's Baby run, though not in the big million-dollar All-American Futurity race. The children were not going. Ric was taking them on a camping trip with their ponies at some creek on the ranch. Barr, she already knew, had a two-day stockmen's conference in Santa Fe. She'd typed up notes for a speech he was scheduled to present Saturday night.

"Why don't you take the weekend off?" Mrs. Chandler suggested to Vickie. "No need for you to sit around here all alone. Why don't you call Lou Ann Wardlow and go shopping in Albuquerque?"

No matter how intimidating Kathy felt Mrs. Chandler to be, she was, Vickie thought a little wryly, totally without class consciousness. She hadn't given a thought to the fact that Lou Ann came from a wealthy ranching family and Vickie was just hired help. To be honest, Vickie doubted that Lou Ann would give that much thought, either. But there were other reasons why the two would hardly care to become chummy.

But all Vickie said was a polite "Thank you. I'll think about it."

Vickie went for a horseback ride after work Thursday evening. She was certain that Barr saw her leave. She was less certain whether she was relieved or disappointed that he did not follow.

She rode the same willing, nonexcitable gelding and headed out toward the old homestead. Once headed that way, the horse needed no direction from her, and she could relax and let her mind wander. She felt that she needed to think, to clear her head in the fresh-scented open air. The sweeping valley and sharply silhouetted mountains to the west had a simplicity and timelessness that she hoped would put her muddled thoughts into proper perspective.

Nothing was as clear-cut as she had assumed it to be when she agreed to come to the ranch. Back at Aunt Verla's, the situation had seemed sharply delineated: Kathy was right, and Ric was wrong. But here everything had gone a little fuzzy, like a photo out of focus. Who *was* right and who wrong?

The answer, Vickie thought uneasily, was probably somewhere between the two sides. Neither Ric nor Kathy was totally right or totally wrong. They were both good and decent but imperfect human beings, people who loved their children very much but who also made very human mistakes.

And here *she* was, caught squarely in the middle, acting as judge and jury. The impossible part of the situation was that she couldn't abandon her task, couldn't simply wash her hands of it and say this is too complicated for me to decide, because that in itself would be a decision. A decision to let Ric keep the children. Without Vickie's help, Kathy hadn't a chance to recover them. Yet depriving Ric of the children he loved wasn't right, either. Two wrongs didn't add up to a right. There was no neutral ground, no happy solution.

And there was the added complication of Barr Chandler, like a wild card thrown into an already unfamiliar deck.

By the time Vickie returned to the corral, she felt physically refreshed, but her thoughts were still in turmoil. She unsaddled the horse and brushed him down, working until his sorrel coat gleamed while her thoughts hammered on.

It all boiled down to one fact, she decided finally. If she did nothing, she was deciding in favor of Ric. If she did what she had come here to do, she was deciding in favor of Kathy. There was no in-between.

Put that way, she knew where her loyalties lay. She had made a commitment to Kathy, and she would keep it. And she must not let her feelings for Barr— whatever they were!—get in the way.

By midday Saturday, the big house was indeed almost empty. Barr had left the night before for his Santa Fe conference. That in itself, Vickie realized unhappily, was enough to make the house feel empty to her. Then Mrs. Chandler's friends picked her up early Saturday morning. Ric and the kids rode out just after lunch, with sleeping bags tied behind their ponies' saddles.

Vickie had let everyone think her own plans were indefinite. Actually, they were not at all indefinite, though she was not particularly proud of them. She knew that Mrs. Chandler used an alcove of her large bedroom as an informal office. Vickie planned to sneak in and see if she could find a calendar or correspondence, *something* that would give some hint about when the visit to Nancy in Phoenix might take place or when some other appointment or event might take the children off the ranch.

She couldn't do it during the day, of course. Doñela was always bustling around. In fact, Doñela took this opportunity to bring the ranch hand's wife, Carol, in to do a top-to-bottom cleaning of Mrs. Chandler's room. Vickie spent the afternoon cleaning her own room, washing out some hand laundry, painting her toenails and restlessly trying not to feel guilty about her nocturnal plans.

She watched television in the den until the eleven o'clock news was over, then tiptoed silently to Doñela's closed door. In frustration, she heard the murmur of voices from within. Doñela was still watching television. Vickie would have to wait a while longer to be safe before creeping into Mrs. Chandler's room.

Vickie went back to her own room. She considered lying down and dozing for a while, but she didn't want to run the risk of sleeping right through the night and missing this ideal opportunity to prowl. She read for a while but couldn't concentrate and found herself growing dangerously sleepy.

A swim would wake her up, she decided impulsively. Quickly, she stripped out of her jeans and into the pink triangles of her bikini. She was halfway tempted to go *au naturel,* but a certain instinctive caution held her back.

Noiselessly, she opened the sliding-glass doors that led from the hallway to the pool. The cool night air hit her with a bite in spite of the towel draped around her body. Quickly, she dropped the towel and slid into the water. Surprisingly, the water felt warmer than the surrounding air, but it was cool enough to dispel any lingering sleepiness.

She sidestroked noiselessly to the opposite end of the pool. The night was gorgeous. A crescent moon curled low over the horizon. Stars beyond number sprinkled the night sky, some boldly glittering, some shining so faintly they seemed to come and go, as if drifting from one dimension to another. Vickie floated dreamily on her back, her restless sense of purpose muted in the pleasure of the night.

A small breeze ruffled the mirror surface, and with it came a small ruffling of Vickie's thoughts. Was Barr looking up at these very same stars—and perhaps sharing them with someone? She knew Hale Wardlow was going to the convention. Would Lou Ann be there, also? Was Barr even now enjoying some pleasure more earthy than a soulful gaze at the moon?

Headlights suddenly arced over the roof of the house. Vickie felt a moment of alarm, then settled back to her float. No doubt just some of the cowboys returning to the bunkhouse after a Saturday night fling.

No, the headlights were moving on to the house. Who could be coming at this hour of the night? Well, if they were guests, they would have to rouse Doñela. Vickie didn't intend to rush to the door in her bikini.

She heard the faint slam of a car door, then silence. She stroked to the shadowed edge of the pool, suddenly wary. And not without reason, she realized suddenly as Barr's tall figure, clad in a western-style business suit, appeared at the outside gate to the pool. He was evidently taking a short cut from the yard to the sliding-glass doors of his bedroom.

Vickie sank as low as possible in the water and clung to the shadowed edge of the pool. He didn't see her . . . good! There was something about meeting Barr under these circumstances that rippled a blend of warning and excitement through her. He was almost to the doors when he stopped and looked back.

Oh, no! Her fallen towel gleamed like a white flag against the dark mosaic tile. He walked over, picked it up and immediately spotted her.

"Wel-l-l, have I been missing something? Do you come out often for a midnight swim?" His devilish smile, startlingly white and infinitely dangerous, flashed in the faint moonlight.

"No! I—I just felt restless tonight," she said defensively. Accusingly, she added, "I thought you were staying in Santa Fe all weekend."

"I gave my speech, and then there didn't seem any real need to stay." He grinned again. "Maybe I was thinking about you, all alone and lonely here at the ranch. . . ." He squatted down beside the edge of the pool and ran his hand over her water-beaded cheek.

Even that slight a touch from him did strange things to her. She shoved herself away from the edge of the pool, the suddenness of her movement splashing a spray of water in his direction. "I'm not lonely!" she protested vehemently.

"You got me all wet." His voice was reproachful. "Now I'll have to come in swimming, too." He made it sound as if one action inevitably followed the other.

"I was just getting out. . . ."

"It won't take me more than a minute to go in and change."

She started to protest, then changed her mind. While he was changing clothes, she would quietly slip away to the safety of her own room. He read her mind as quickly and accurately as if she had blared her intentions over a loudspeaker.

"But you won't be here when I return, will you? In that case—" He tossed his briefcase to a redwood lounge chair and stripped off his jacket.

His hands were on his belt buckle before Vickie gathered her wits together sufficiently to gasp, "What are you *doing?*"

"Going swimming. And since you won't give me time to go in and get my suit . . ." The belt was undone, the shirt tail hanging. His deft fingers rapidly attacked the buttons closing the shirt.

"Go get your suit!" Thank heaven, she thought, she hadn't given in to her own small impulse to swim in the nude!

"You'll be here when I return?"

"Yes. . . ."

"Say it as if you mean it!"

"Yes! I'll be here."

"You'd better be," he warned.

Vicki treaded water while he strode to the dark sliding-glass doors. A moment later, a light flashed on, and she could see a shadowy outline of his figure moving around inside. She hesitated. What could he do if she reneged on her promise and wasn't here when he returned? *Nothing,* she told herself defiantly.

And yet she wasn't at all sure that was true. She had the uneasy feeling Barr was rather resourceful, and she wasn't sure she had the courage to test those resources. Or his determination. While she was still trying to decide if she dared sneak away, he reappeared in the doorway, a dark towel tied around his waist.

Vickie stared at him suspiciously. She wasn't certain there were swim trunks beneath that towel. He smiled at her, knowing full well what she was thinking.

"I thought about it," he agreed. He whipped off the towel. "But I didn't do it."

He was wearing a brief, white swim suit, tautly molded to the underlying muscle. He dove smoothly from the edge of the pool, his body cutting the water cleanly and almost silently. Vickie gasped as he came up beside her, his hands touching first her feet and then gliding up the length of her body.

"You'd better swim to keep warm," he said. "Your skin is all goose bumpy."

"I'm not cold."

That was all too true. The prickle of her skin came from something else. She was hardly conscious of the water around her, couldn't have said if it was hot or cold. The faint moonlight sheened his skin with silver. A dark shadow of hair fell across his forehead. He flung it back with a stallion toss of his head, showering her with droplets. A pagan water god, she thought with a breathless sense of unreality. His muscular arms and legs encircled her with sinewy strength.

Then he laughed, breaking that magical spell but creating another even more dangerous one, because she laughed back, and there was nothing to laugh about except the sheer joy and excitement of being there together.

She twisted away from him, and they played a wild game that was part tag, part hide-and-seek, part pure man-woman temptation. Under and above water they dipped and rose like dolphins, circling, turning, gliding silently, splashing noisily. She lost him in the dark waters, found him again when he glided between her outstretched legs.

"We're going to wake Doñela!" Vickie gasped, pausing to grab the side of the pool and catch her breath.

"Doñela sleeps like a log." He smoothed her dripping hair away from her face. "Maybe I've been mistaken," he said huskily. "Maybe you're a mermaid instead of a wildcat." His hand slid to her waist, arching her body to his.

The warm intimacy of his voice alarmed her, and the touch of his lean body beneath the water heightened that alarm to siren signals of warning.

"I'd better go inside."

"Not yet . . ." His hand slid lower, curving her body ever more intimately against his.

She gave a sudden, panicky lunge, intending to use her feet to push herself away from the edge and escape him, but her foot slipped, and she came up sputtering and gasping. Her foot hurt where it had scraped against the side of the pool.

"What happened?"

"Nothing." She grabbed the metal ladder and climbed out of the pool. In the dying moonlight, the blood welling to the surface of the broken skin on her foot looked dark and ominous.

He pulled himself lithely out of the pool behind her and peered at the scrape. "We'd better get something on that."

"Really, it's nothing. Just a little scratch."

"But it was my fault." He leaned over and swept her into his arms in one powerful swoop. "I don't want you suing the ranch for blood poisoning or something. We'll put some antiseptic on it."

"Put me down!" She kicked her feet wildly but impotently, because his clamped grip held her immobilized above the knees. "I'm perfectly capable of walking to my room by myself!"

"And do you have medical equipment there?" he inquired.

"I don't need major surgery!"

"That means you don't have anything to put on it, do you? Then I'll take you to my room. I have Band-Aids and antiseptic."

He carried her to the sliding-glass door and managed to open it and turn on a light without releasing his hold on her. He deposited her in an easy chair, disappeared into the adjoining bathroom and returned with a small first-aid kit a bare moment later, as if suspicious she might try to sneak out. He carefully cleaned the scraped skin with antiseptic.

While he worked, Vickie took a quick inventory of the room. It was considerably more luxurious than her own but unmistakably masculine. There was a fireplace in one corner, a pueblo type with smoothly curved lines and a small, arched opening. A collection of antique silver spurs decorated one wall. The carpet felt soft and lush under her bare feet, and she was uncomfortably aware of dampness around her on the velvet chair. Barr didn't seem concerned, however.

The antiseptic was stinging, and she winced. "Where did you get your medical training, doctor?" she asked tartly.

"In the barn, practicing on cattle." He looked up, his eyes dancing wickedly. Jewel droplets of water clung to his smoothly muscled shoulders and glittered on his eyelashes. "However, I'm glad I graduated to this type of work. You don't kick, and the anatomy is decidedly more interesting."

"Don't be too sure I don't kick," she warned.

He applied a soothing cream after the antiseptic. They were both aware that the small scrape hardly required this much solicitous attention, but Vickie found herself going along with the pretense that it did.

"Sometimes you puzzle me," she said slowly. He was bending over her foot, chestnut hair highlighted with gold in the lamplight, naked shoulders gleaming. She had to restrain herself from running her fingers through the crisp hair or over the bronzed skin.

He looked up. "The feeling is mutual." A certain meaningful inflection spiced his light comment. Vickie flushed, knowing full well he meant that her ambivalent physical reaction to him sometimes puzzled him.

She refused to acknowledge that she caught his hinted meaning, however. "In fact, all of you Chandlers rather puzzle me," she enlarged.

"In what way?" His head dipped again to the task at hand. Her pink-painted toenails looked incongruously frivolous under his strong, competent hands.

"Your mother seems at home on the ranch. And yet sometimes I have the feeling—"

"My mother came from Philadelphia. Very proper family. Proper girls' school. Proper university education. Her knowledge of livestock was limited to an ability to distinguish between a horse and a cow. *If* they weren't too far away." He laughed. "I understand her family was horrified when she came out here to visit a school friend, fell in love and never went home."

"And managed to run the ranch after your father's death."

"She didn't have an easy time of it," he agreed. He plastered a Band-Aid over the scratch and eyed the result critically.

"And you quit school to help after she got hurt."

"I didn't have much choice."

"But you don't seem—" She paused, wondering if she was prying too far in her curiosity.

He laughed again. "I may have missed out on the formal education my brothers received, but my mother wasn't about to let me remain totally ignorant just because I was running the ranch. I thought I was pretty important stuff all day, bossing the men around and making big decisions, but in the evening I had to sit by my mother's side while she drilled everything from Shakespeare to Greek history into me." He tilted his head, his gaze turned inward on that not unpleasant memory of the past. But his hand still had a firm grip on her foot. "I rather resented it at the time, of course. It all seemed irrelevant. But now . . . Well, I enjoy country and western music, but I'm glad she taught me to appreciate a symphony, too."

He looked down at Vickie's foot as if he had momentarily forgotten he was holding it. He lifted it, inspected instep, arch and slim ankle almost clinically, and then he slowly and deliberately kissed the sensitive curve of the arch.

A fire-and-ice shiver raced through Vickie. She gave a small, in-drawn gasp of breath, feeling as if that particular portion of her foot were connected to every nerve in her body and each one had suddenly become exquisitely alive.

"You're cold," he said.

"No. . . ." She looked in surprise at her prickled skin. A shiver trembled through her. Cold? Perhaps. . . .

He tossed a short, blue velour robe to her. "Put that on."

The robe fell across her lap. She was suddenly conscious of her near nakedness. Here in the privacy of Barr's bedroom, the pink triangles seemed to cover even less than they did in water and sunshine. Yet there was something almost terrifyingly intimate about putting on the robe that usually enclosed his hard, masculine body. She stood up suddenly, grabbing for the robe as it started to slide toward the floor.

"I'd better be going."

He took the robe from her suddenly nerveless hands and draped it around her shoulders. He pulled the front tightly shut, trapping her arms against her body, and then used his grip on the robe to pull her to him.

His mouth dipped to hers, lips tenderly soft and yet at the same time powerful, as if some latent strength lay behind them, in reserve if needed. Vickie melted under the seductive softness of his kiss and the rough-tender possession of his tongue. Her arms were bound to her sides beneath the robe, but her hands strained to press her finger tips against the taut, hard muscles of his thighs.

"I missed you, do you know that? I was away from the ranch for one night, and I missed you." He sounded halfway resentful, his usual good-humored, teasing tone missing. His gaze lingered on her mouth.

"Is that why you came back?"

"Maybe." His hands released their grip on the robe and slid under the soft material to the bare skin of her waist, pulling her more intimately against him.

The touch felt like fire on her skin. He propelled her backward with gentle but irresistible force until she sprawled across the wide bed. His lithe body followed hers, landing beside her on the bed with one leg flung over hers.

"We're all wet!" she protested. "We're getting your bed all wet. . . ." A foolish protest, she realized even as she said the words, angry with herself. Why didn't she protest being pushed to his bed and held there with silken strength? Why had she let him carry her in here? She had known he would hold and kiss her. But she hadn't admitted that to herself, had gone along with the injured-foot charade. Why? Because she wanted him to hold and kiss her. . . .

He ran his fingers lightly over the smooth, taut skin above her bikini bottom. "Your skin is almost dry. Only our suits are wet. So . . ." His finger tips edged beneath the narrow band of pink material encircling her hips.

She grabbed his hand. "No!" Another moment and he'd have had the damp pink triangle tangled somewhere around her ankles. "Don't do that!"

He slid over her, a smile tilting his mouth as he looked down at her. "Somehow I knew you'd do that." The smoky smolder in his eyes belied the wry resignation in his voice. His finger tip traced the curve of her mouth, and then his lips followed, outlining her mouth with a whisper of feathery kisses from corner to corner, melting her protests before they could form into words.

The top of her bikini had twisted as he slid over her, and her bare breasts were pressed against the solid, warm wall of his naked chest. He moved gently, savoring the contact.

"Do you know I lie over here alone at night, wishing you were with me?" he whispered. "And now you're here, and I know you want me as much as I want you. Yet you're fighting it because of something that happened in the past, something that had nothing to do with me."

Oh, yes, a battle was raging within Vickie, a silent, motionless war between the awakening desires of her body and the warning resistance of her mind. But the resistance had so little to work with, so little to strengthen it, and her desires were bombarded from all sides with sensual encouragement. The feel of his lean, masculine body molded against the feminine curves and hollows of hers. The sound of his ragged breathing mingled with her own. The taste of his mouth and the scent of his damp hair and skin, more intoxicating than any cologne.

But he was wrong about one thing, she thought wildly. The battle had everything to do with him, and her resistance was weakening. She could no longer hold herself totally motionless. Her arms crept around him, and her body made a small, instinctive movement of desire against his.

"I want to love you," he whispered softly. "I want to show you that love can be beautiful and healing instead of hurting. I want to love away whatever happened to you in the past. . . ."

Chapter Six

He kissed her again, and his lean body possessed her with an intimacy that was little short of total. Even with her lack of experience, Vickie recognized that they were rapidly approaching a point of no return, a point beyond which passion would sweep away all barriers of reason and logic, bury all caution in a landslide of desire.

Her body and mind were sending conflicting messages. Yes, she wanted him! No, she must not let herself become involved with him! And the cynical inner retort came back that the battle was a little late; she was already involved. She was in his room, on his bed, her body enveloped in his passionate embrace and her emotions stretched to the breaking point by desire and something above and beyond simple physical yearning. And the only end to which it could lead, the inevitable conclusion, was heartbreak.

Run the risk of heartbreak, her treacherous, willful body demanded recklessly!

Yes. . . .

But she couldn't run the risk of betraying Kathy and Aunt Verla. Again, the granite truth hit her: if she made love with Barr, he would know she had lied about a previous marriage. And once one lie was exposed,

Barr would relentlessly strip away all the lies and secrets. He had that hard inner core of ruthlessness and steel determination that would drive him until he uncovered everything. She must not let that happen! She must not let physical desire triumph over her loyalty to her family. She must keep up the pretense she had created.

"Barr . . ." She twisted beneath him, removing her arms from around him and trying to wedge her clenched fists between their tightly welded bodies.

"Am I hurting you?" He lifted himself on one elbow, instantly contrite. He looked down at her and smiled fondly. "Let's get out of these wet suits."

"No!" She used the small separation to sandwich her hands between them and break the all-enveloping contact, though she could still feel the fine, crisp hair on his chest against her exposed breasts and the solid muscles of his thighs against her legs.

His gaze narrowed, but his expression was more puzzled than angry. "Would you rather go to your room?"

"Yes!" She instantly realized that was the wrong answer. He was not suggesting that she go to her room *alone*. "No!" she corrected. That wasn't right, either! That sounded as if she wanted to stay here. She took a deep, steadying breath. "What I mean is, I—I want—I mean, I'm going to my room. Alone."

"You can't mean that! Not *now*." His half-astonished, half-angry word *now* took in the intimate contact of their bodies on the big bed and the passion that mounted like a rising flame between them.

"Yes, I do mean it. You told me I could say a . . . a 'simple no' and you would respect it and be patient, and that's what I'm saying. A simple *no*."

He rolled away from her, one arm outstretched, the other flung across his eyes. His damp, naked chest rose and fell in great, surging breaths. She knew a battle now raged within *him*. On one side was desire and the inescapable knowledge that with his greater strength he could force himself on her—and the suspicion that under present circumstances her resistance would undoubtedly crumble with very little force involved. On the other side of the battle was his promise to be patient and understanding, to accept her "simple no."

Finally, he turned over on his side, his head braced on one hand. "You do know how to try a man's patience to the utmost, don't you?" His voice wasn't shaky, but it betrayed his tremendous effort at self-control. His smile was ragged, as if perhaps he regretted what he had said that day they rode to the homestead together.

"I didn't mean to—to try your patience," Vickie said. She rearranged her disheveled bathing suit. "It's just that—"

"I know." He stroked her face lightly, the small tremor of his hand revealing the effort he still had to exert to hold his desires in check. He looked both frustrated and perplexed. "What *did* he do to you, Vickie, to make you so afraid of love?"

Afraid? Yes! Vickie thought wildly. But not of what he thought. And it wasn't *love* he was offering, anyway, she thought scornfully. It was sex, pure and simple. When she made no reply, his hand descended to her bare shoulder, the touch not quite as gentle as before.

"I hope I'm not wrong about you, my little wildcat-kitten," he said, his voice suddenly soft with danger.

"Wr-wrong? In what way?" She felt a surge of pure panic. Did he know . . . suspect . . . ?

"Sometimes I wonder if you don't rather enjoy putting a man through somersaults and cartwheels. Maybe you're just a little tease who gets a certain pleasure out of leading a man on and then saying *no* at the last minute. Maybe you plan to make every man in your future pay for what one did in the past."

Vickie was aghast at the accusations. "No!"

"And sometimes I think *no* is your favorite word," he added grimly.

She sat up, furiously intending to stalk out, and instead found herself entangled in the velour robe he had earlier draped around her. She kicked angrily at the rope cord caught around her ankle. He thrust a rigid arm in front of her shoulders.

"Vickie—"

"Let go of me!"

He forced her down against the bed again, controlling her frantic struggles with both the strength of his grip and weight of his body. She saw the passion still smoldering in his eyes, read the powerful inclination to ignore her struggles and protests. Suddenly, she lay very still, knowing this was out of her control.

"I want you as I've never wanted any woman in my life," he said huskily.

She didn't reply, could only look at him wide-eyed.

"Stay with me tonight," he pleaded softly. "Nothing will happen. I promise. Just stay with me and let me hold you."

"Could you—do that?" she asked wonderingly.

He kissed her on the end of her nose. "Do you doubt my will power?" he challenged lightly.

No, truthfully she didn't, she thought as she searched his sage-green eyes with her own, darkened by emotion. He would live up to his word. But she wasn't so positive about the strength of her own will power.

"Please?" he asked. He sounded almost boyish and solemnly repeated his promise. "Nothing will happen. I just want to hold you."

Minutes later, they were snuggled together under the covers of his big bed, heads on the same pillow. His body curved around hers, one hand cupping her breast tenderly.

"Comfortable?" His voice was a warm, intimate murmur against her hair.

Comfortable? Oh, yes, she thought fervently. But she'd never be able to sleep, not with the newness of a male body next to her in bed. This wasn't fair to him, she thought, feeling a moment of guilt. Making him bear the brunt of self-control, making him exert his will power while she simply luxuriated in the warm wonder of lying next to him.

Then, a few moments later, she realized from the soft regularity of his breathing that he was asleep. She felt a small flurry of indignation. Sleeping! And then she had to laugh at herself, and before long she slept, too.

She woke once in the night to find they had changed position. Her body was spooned around his now, her knees tucked into the angle of his. And then she slept again, sweetly, dreamlessly.

The next time she woke, they were back to their former position, his body curved warmly around hers. A pink-silver dawn light permeated the room. Barr was awake.

"I'd better get back to my own room." She said it with regret, reluctant to move away from the delicious warmth of his body.

"So soon?" He wound a tendril of her dark hair around his finger and tickled her cheek with it. "How did you sleep?"

"Fine." She turned her head to look back over her shoulder at him. His chestnut hair was tousled, his green eyes smoky warm. "How about you?"

"I can think of just one small improvement that would have made the night perfect." He grinned wickedly, leaned forward and nibbled her ear lobe lightly.

The touch sent a delicious tingle through Vickie, and she reacted by scrambling out of bed. "May I borrow this?" she asked, hastily picking up the blue velour robe.

"By all means." He slid out the other side of the bed and slipped a pair of faded jeans over his long legs.

Vickie felt suddenly awkward as she headed for the sliding-glass door, the oversized robe dangling around her. What did she say now? Somehow "Thanks for the lovely evening" didn't seem quite appropriate.

He took care of the awkward moment. He put an arm around her shoulders and went to the door with her. "I'll see you at breakfast, okay?"

She nodded. He slid the door open. The air smelled gloriously fresh and dewy. The sunrise sky was the color of rose petals and lilacs. A bird, surprised in an early-morning bath in the children's wading pool, fluttered skyward.

Barr let her take a step, then whirled her back to face him. "You see?" he said softly, all trace of teasing and lightness gone. "Nothing happened."

He cupped her chin with his hand and kissed her on the mouth. It was a tender kiss, almost unbearably sweet, and yet the banked fires of passion smoldered behind it. Yes, he had lived up to his promise, she thought tremulously. It was a victory of mind over body, will power over physical passion, because she was exquisitely aware that the desire had not left his body.

Then in an abrupt change of mood, he gave her a playful swat on the bottom. "Back to your room, woman, before my will power and patience expire in a puff of smoke."

Vickie scampered around the pool and entered the other wing of the house through the door she had exited last night. Was it really only last night? Moments later, she was in her room, peering through a crack in the drapes at Barr's closed door.

She felt strange, lightheaded. She let the drape fall and turned back to the room. The mirror showed the reflection of a woman who looked familiar, yet different. Glowing. Radiant. Vital. What Barr had done was somehow more meaningful than the wildest passion, the most ecstatic lovemaking. He had given his promise that nothing would happen, and he had lived up to the vow and held her with warmth and tenderness.

But even as she looked at the figure in the mirror, the glow dimmed, the exuberance faded. Her hand went to her mouth in shock. The radiant green eyes in the mirror darkened in dismay. Barr said nothing had happened, but he was wrong. *Wrong!* Something had happened, something cataclysmic and unthinkable. She had done the one thing she must not do: she had fallen in love with him.

Fallen in love with Barr Chandler.

No!

But it was true. And it was a hopeless situation. Nothing could ever come of it.

Now she felt more dazed than lightheaded. She showered, but there seemed a wall between her skin and the hot needles of water. Last night her skin had been ultrasensitive, alive to each tiny nuance of Barr's touch. But this morning the sensitive nerves were wooden and dead.

What now? she wondered wildly. Meet him at breakfast, act as if nothing had happened? No, she couldn't. Hastily, she threw on jeans and T-shirt, grabbed her car keys and raced outside.

She drove toward Albuquerque, knowing nowhere

else to go. She spent the day in a frantic race of activity, dashing from one local attraction to another. The Indian Pueblo Cultural Center. The Albuquerque Museum. A ride up the Sandia Peak Aerial Tramway, the pleasure of the ride and the magnificence of the view lost on her. In between, she grabbed a hamburger, and in the evening she saw a movie.

Belatedly, she realized that by spending the night with Barr, she had sabotaged her chances to snoop for information in Mrs. Chandler's room. Her feelings on that point were mixed. Guilt because she had put her own pleasure before her duty to Kathy and Aunt Verla and the kids. But a twinge of relief, too, because she hated sneaking and snooping.

It was almost midnight by the time she returned to the ranch. The house, including Barr's room, was dark. She opened the door to her room, halfway surprised to find everything just as she had left it. She felt so changed that it seemed the room should also have changed.

During the day, she had, if nothing else, managed to wear herself out. She dropped into bed exhausted, her mind numb. She plunged immediately into a heavy, unsatisfying sleep, and she woke in the morning feeling as weary as when she went to bed. Her head felt thick and heavy, her body achy and listless.

Cautiously, she sorted out her feelings and examined them, hoping against hope that she had been mistaken. She wasn't in love, she told herself. What she had felt yesterday morning was just a foolish euphoria, a gratitude that Barr hadn't relentlessly forced or seduced her.

She immediately knew that hope was as phony as the web of lies she had woven around herself. She was in love with him.

She skipped breakfast and went directly to the office,

thinking that if she got there before Barr, she would somehow put herself in a less vulnerable position. She was too late. He was already there.

His eyes appraised her, cutting through the makeup she had applied to hide the shadows under her eyes. If he was angry, he concealed it well. If he felt *anything*, he concealed it.

All he said was a wary "I didn't see you at breakfast yesterday."

She lifted her head defiantly and deliberately gave her dark hair a toss. "I decided to take a drive."

"I see."

And that was all that was said. He studied her a few moments longer, his expression inscrutable. That damned all-powerful self-control again, she thought a little wildly. Then he brusquely named some figures and reports he needed out of the files, and she briskly set about locating them.

He left the office at about ten o'clock and didn't return. When she realized that he wasn't coming back, she put her arms down on the typewriter and weakly leaned her head against them. How long could she keep this up, acting cool and aloof, when she longed to fling her arms around him and tell him she loved him? He'd respond—she knew he would! He'd fold her in his arms. . . .

And where would they go from there? she reminded herself bitterly. Oh, if only she could get this over with; if only she could see some end in sight! The end of loving him? No, that would take longer, much longer. But if she could just end the ordeal of seeing him every day, do her duty and somehow put all this behind her!

The chance came sooner than she expected. At dinner, Mrs. Chandler remarked casually that she thought this coming weekend would be a good time to take Benji and Susan over to visit Nancy in Phoenix. Nancy wanted to give a little birthday party for Benji. Just as casually, Barr agreed that he had some ranch and feed-lot figures he wanted to coordinate with Niles, and he could take care of that at the same time. They would leave shortly after lunch on Friday.

Vickie debated calling Kathy immediately but decided against it. She first needed to find out Nancy's address in Phoenix, plus some sort of weekend schedule that would help Kathy and her hired helper figure out a workable plan for snatching the kids. She went about the tasks with a grim determination. She had wanted to get this over with, yet now the time was racing away from her all too quickly. Her plan was to make her getaway from the ranch immediately after Barr, Mrs. Chandler and the children took off in the plane for Phoenix on Friday. After that moment, she would never see Barr again unless it was in some courtroom confrontation with her on Kathy's side and Barr on Ric's side. The pain of loss was an ache that permeated body, mind and soul.

Locating Nancy's address proved easy enough. It was in the address book Barr kept in his office desk drawer. Finding out a schedule for the family's activities in Phoenix was more difficult. Barr seemed unapproachable as a fortress, so Vickie decided she'd have to try to worm some information out of Mrs. Chandler. Before she could do that, Barr dropped a bombshell just as he was leaving the office Wednesday.

"By the way, you'll have to fly to Phoenix with us Friday. I'll need you along when I discuss figures with Niles." He looked at her through narrowed eyes, as if challenging her to refuse.

She stared at him in dismay. She couldn't go to Phoenix! Everything was going to blow sky high when the children were snatched there. She couldn't be in Phoenix when it happened, with her car and belongings all here on the ranch.

"Have you some objection?" he prodded.

"Isn't the plane too small to carry all of us?"

"It's a four-seater. There'll be room."

"But surely I could look up all the figures you need and give them to you before you go. Or you could call me here," she added with sudden inspiration and a brightly forced smile.

"No. I want you there." He did not smile.

She had the sudden intuition that his demand that she go to Phoenix was not entirely a business matter. What did that mean? Her heart gave a tumultuous flip-flop. She felt a surge of hope and just as quickly a droop of despair. There was no hope.

"I'll expect you to be ready by noon Friday," he said crisply. He ended the brief discussion with another command. "There won't be room for heavy luggage but bring something dressy."

Vickie telephoned Kathy that afternoon and gave her the news, wishing she could feel more elated about it. All she felt was a numb dread, a growing apprehension that somehow this was all going to end in terrible tragedy, that no one would come out a winner, least of all Vickie herself.

"So you'll call me again when you get to Phoenix?" Kathy said, running over the plans again.

"Yes. Friday night. I know that means a long, hard drive to Phoenix for you, but I just haven't been able to find out any more here except that Barr doesn't plan to fly back to the ranch until late Sunday afternoon."

"Kitten, what are you going to do?" Kathy asked in sudden alarm, as if she just that moment realized in what a predicament this put Vickie.

"I'm not sure yet. Don't worry," Vickie said with considerably more assurance than she felt. "I'll think of something."

"Maybe you ought to just jump in the car and come with us when we grab the kids," Kathy suggested.

"No. I think I'll try to bluff it through until I can get back to the ranch and pick up my car and things. But you have to promise me one thing, Kath." Vickie's voice was suddenly intense. "There's one thing you *must* do."

"What's that?"

"You have to call and let the Chandlers know you have Benji and Susan. And you have to do it just as soon as you possibly can so they'll know nothing terrible has happened to them."

"Ric didn't call me for three days when he took Benji and Susan!"

"I know. But this is different. You knew he had the kids. The Chandlers aren't going to know unless you call and tell them that Benji and Susan haven't really been kidnaped or murdered or something horrible. And they love them, Kath. They really do. Even Barr. It wouldn't be fair to let them think the worst."

"Okay," Kathy finally agreed reluctantly. "I'll call them as soon as I'm sure we're safely away."

"Promise?"

"Promise. But I won't tell them where we are."

"I wouldn't expect that." Vickie tried to keep out of her voice the heaviness she felt. She had the unhappy feeling that a trap was inexorably tightening around her as well as around the Chandlers.

The plane took off on schedule shortly after lunch Friday. Vickie rode up front with Barr, Mrs. Chandler and the children in the rear seat. Vickie wore comfortable linen slacks and a cool, casual blouse. She had packed a jade-green gown, dressy but crush resistant, though she still wasn't certain why she needed something dressy.

In spite of her nervousness and dread over what only she knew lay ahead this weekend, Vickie couldn't escape a certain exhilaration as the plane roared down the dirt airstrip and climbed into the cloudless sky. Barr handled the plane as he did almost everything, with assurance, expertise and efficiency.

Vickie was fascinated by the immense landscape sprawled below them. From above, the flat valleys were a great tan sea separated by ridges of mountains pushed up from below by some cataclysmic force. They drowsed like great, half-buried prehistoric beasts under the blazing sun. There was the silvery ribbon of the Rio Grande, cultivated fields, then barren mountains and deserts. After the first few minutes, Benji and Susan, like most children, weren't all that interested in the awe-inspiring scenery below. Mrs. Chandler kept them busy with coloring books and games. The noise of the plane was not conducive to conversation, and dialogue between Vickie and Barr was limited to pointing out something interesting below. There was a tension between them, as there had been all week, that perhaps inhibited conversation even more than the engine noise.

The first thing of which Vickie was aware when they landed in Phoenix was the heat. In August, midafternoon Phoenix roasted. Baked. Sizzled. The sky had a blue-white incandescence, and heat waves danced and rippled on the airport runway.

Before Vickie had time to wilt, however, Nancy whisked them off in her air-conditioned Cadillac. Nancy was petite and vivacious, and she scooped up Benji and Susan as if she could hardly wait to get her hands on them. She treated Vickie with warm friendliness, saying she was so glad Vickie had come along, and Vickie had no doubt that she sincerely meant it. Vickie tried to quell a growing distaste for what she had to do, resolutely reminding herself that even if these were perfectly marvelous people, so long as they had the kids, Kathy and Aunt Verla did *not* have them. And Kathy and Aunt Verla loved and wanted Benji and Susan desperately, too.

Nancy's home was large and sprawling. Vickie guessed that it had been meant for a big family, but the extra space was used instead for entertaining house guests. There was an oval swimming pool and extensive desert-style landscaping with cactus and boulders. And comfortable air conditioning, of course, within the house. Vickie's room was surprisingly decorated with attractive French antique furniture, but the first thing she noted was the phone by the bedside. One problem already solved. She could make her important call to Kathy in privacy, needing only to time the call so that someone else wasn't likely to pick up another extension. Now she just had to figure out the best time for the snatch. She hadn't planned and definitely did not *want* to be this closely involved, but there was no escaping it now.

Nancy's husband, Bill, turned out to be as likable as his wife. Darn, Vickie thought ruefully. Why couldn't these people be proper ogres and villains? Niles and Serena came over, and dinner was a casual, relaxed affair for everyone but Vickie, whose appetite was nil. The big topic of conversation was Amanda's Baby and the big All-American Futurity race coming up over the Labor Day weekend. The entire family was planning to congregate in Ruidoso for it. They were actually all joint owners of the race horse, but Mrs. Chandler was most personally involved because she had hand

113

raised the filly. They were all concerned because the filly, though she had won the race Mrs. Chandler had gone down to watch, had pulled up lame afterward.

Then the needed bits of information about the weekend schedule fell neatly into Vickie's lap. Nancy was giving her little birthday party for Benji tomorrow afternoon. Saturday evening, all the adults would attend a dinner party at the home of some friends. The children, for a few hours, would be in the house alone with a baby sitter. And that, Vickie thought grimly, should be sufficient opportunity for Kathy's experienced friend to pull off a successful snatch. Rescue, Vickie mentally corrected herself, although at the moment the word Kathy always used seemed almost absurd. Vickie and Barr were scheduled to spend all day Saturday with Niles on business, then go to Niles and Serena's home for the night and attend the dinner party from there.

Only Vickie knew that the happy Sunday dinner they were all scheduled to share at Nancy and Bill's "best steak house in Phoenix" would probably never come off. It was as if two separate plays were carefully choreographed for the same time and space, one the Chandlers', one Kathy's and her helper's, and they were going to collide and explode in midstage. And Vickie was going to be caught in the middle.

The day had actually been too hot for comfortable swimming, but after dinner everyone decided to take a dip in the pool. Nancy loaned Vickie a one-piece suit that was cut along flattering but rather conservative lines. Vickie swam for a few minutes, then stretched out in a webbed lounge chair. The evening air was still hot.

Barr, wearing tan-gold swim trunks that came close to blending with his sun-bronzed skin, casually wandered over. Or perhaps he merely made it appear casual.

He perched on the edge of another chair, iced drink in one hand. "Enjoying yourself?"

"Yes, of course." Vickie spoke with a forced brightness. "Nancy and Bill are marvelous people, and they have a lovely home."

He regarded her thoughtfully. "You seem a little tense and nervous," he observed, all too correctly.

Was that merely a casual comment or a warning that he suspected something? She started to take a sip from her own drink, realized that her hand had a giveaway tremble and clutched the arm of the chair instead. Desperately, she searched for some different, safer topic of conversation.

"I was surprised when I met Nancy." Vickie struggled to maintain that artificial brightness. "She and Niles don't look at all like twins."

One chestnut eyebrow tilted. "How did you happen to know they *are* twins?"

Because Kathy had told her, of course, Vickie realized in sudden panic. "I—I don't know. Someone must have mentioned it, I suppose." But now that she thought about it, Vickie was almost certain that the fact had *not* been mentioned by anyone at the ranch. In her eagerness to get away from one dangerous subject, she had evidently blundered into another. "Why do you ask?" she asked, trying to put him in the defensive position of answering questions rather than asking them.

He shrugged. "It's just something that isn't usually mentioned. Because of some health problems, Niles entered school a year later than Nancy. He was always uncomfortable and self-conscious about being a year behind, so the twin status between them was just

115

ignored. It carried over even after they became adults. Not many people outside the family know they're twins except for a few old-timers in the valley who remember when they were born, I suppose."

"Well, someone at the ranch must have mentioned it to me," Vickie said, standing her ground stubbornly.

"I suppose."

He was looking at her with that intensity that made her feel as if he stripped away the protective covering over every private thought she had, every secret she hid. And the inspection was pretty good at stripping away the bathing suit, too, she thought angrily, feeling suddenly exposed in body as well as mind.

She stood up. "I'm going to bed."

"It's early yet."

"I'm going to bed," she repeated stubbornly.

In her room, Vickie showered to wash away any lingering trace of pool chemicals, then settled down to wait until she could safely place her call. The minutes crawled by. The weekend was going to be endless, she realized despairingly. How was she ever going to get through it? Working with Barr all day, attending a dinner party, bluffing and pretending until somehow she could escape after Kathy got the kids. And if Barr realized her part in the conspiracy before she could get away . . . She shuddered.

She heard muffled sounds from the room next door. Barr's room. Her despair increased. How was she ever going to get through *tonight*?

Each night she was tormented by the memory of that night with Barr. There had been a sweet luxury to sleeping in his arms that made her feel bereft, cheated of something infinitely precious when she slept alone in her bed.

Finally, the house settled into silence. Quietly, wondering uneasily if a voice could be heard from one room to the next, Vickie went through the by-now familiar procedure of making the collect call to Amarillo.

To her astonishment, Kathy instantly burst into tears. It took several tries for Vickie to get out of her exactly what had happened. The hired child snatcher had hurt his foot and was hospitalized for the next four days. They would have to pass up this weekend's golden opportunity.

"Kitten, I'm almost tempted to try it alone," Kathy blubbered. "It's Benji's *birthday*. Mom and I were so counting on having them home by his birthday."

"I know, hon." Vickie sympathized with Kathy's desperation, but Kathy was obviously in no emotional state to try something as vital and tricky as this alone. She needed her experienced hired helper. "But we'll just have to be patient."

Kathy cried some more, and Vickie soothed her, promising there would be future opportunities. For Kathy's sake, Vickie was sorry this had happened. Her hopes had soared so high, only to be cruelly dashed.

But for herself, Vickie suddenly felt like a condemned prisoner who had gotten an unexpected reprieve. Nothing was going to happen this weekend, after all! She wanted to shout it to the world. She wouldn't yet have to flee from the ranch like some thief in the night, wouldn't yet have to feel the agony of Barr's fury and hatred or the knowledge that she would never see him again.

She felt alive, free, giddy with relief. The condemned prisoner had a few more days to live!

Chapter Seven

Vickie slept dreamlessly and woke gloriously rested and refreshed, as if a crushing weight had been lifted from her. She felt so light, so free!

She knew the reprieve was only temporary, of course. Once back at the New Mexico ranch, she must start searching for another chink in the Chandlers' armor. But just for this weekend she need not give it another thought, and the relief was deliciously sweet. She felt a little giddy, charged up, and the mirror showed a brilliance in her green eyes. A smile danced around her mouth even as she tried to keep her lips demure and prim.

Breakfast was on the patio. The day was already warm; the pool was delightful. Sunlight reflected off the water with a dazzling glitter. Last night, Vickie had merely pushed her food around on her plate, but this morning she downed ham, eggs and cinnamon rolls with a voracious appetite. In spite of Barr's statement that today would be devoted to business with Niles, he seemed in no hurry to get to it. He kept giving Vickie curious little glances, as if he couldn't figure out what had happened to her between last night and this morning.

"You must have gotten a good night's sleep," he

suggested finally. "You're positively glowing this morning."

"Oh, yes, a marvelous night's sleep!" Vickie agreed quickly.

He lifted the coffeepot questioningly, and she nodded her head. Coffee had never tasted more rich and flavorful than it did on this glorious morning. She felt like dancing around the pool. Nothing terrible was going to happen this weekend!

"Anything special you'd like to do here in Phoenix?" Barr asked casually.

"I was under the impression that I came along to work," Vickie observed. The words came out tart but lighthearted rather than severely reproving, as she had intended them.

Barr scowled, but he couldn't hold back the twitch of a grin, as if he suspected he'd been caught. "All work and no play—" he began.

"Just means you have more income tax to pay," Vickie finished frivolously.

Barr laughed outright. They were alone on the patio by then. Nancy and Mrs. Chandler had gone inside to decorate for Benji's birthday party, and Bill had left for the restaurant. Barr leaned over and ran his hand lightly over her cheek and throat.

"Then we might as well play." His hand tightened slightly on the slender curve of her throat, pulling her toward him. His gaze was on her mouth. "Vickie—"

"How's the coffeepot doing?" Nancy called cheerily from the pass-through window to the kitchen. "Need a refill?"

Barr groaned lightly. "My sister and her incredible timing," he muttered. To his sister he called, "No thanks, Nance."

"I didn't see anything so bad about her timing," Vickie said innocently. Barr leaned toward Vickie

119

again, smoldering intent in his eyes, but Benji and Susan raced out in swim suits. They started a noisy and rather original version of shuffleboard on the court alongside the pool.

"We have a whole weekend ahead of us. There won't always be someone around to interrupt," Barr warned.

"Promises, promises," Vickie teased with mischievous recklessness.

Barr made an attempt to scowl ferociously, but her bubbly mood was infectious, and he laughed instead.

Vickie picked up the breakfast dishes and carried them inside, while Barr joined the children in their game. The sounds of their happy laughter gave Vickie's heart a momentary wrench, but she resolutely put it aside. Just for this weekend she would not think of duty . . . or loss. Or responsibility . . . or painful endings somewhere out in the future. Just for now she was free and alive and suddenly looking forward to the weekend with happy anticipation instead of dread.

Vickie repacked her overnight case, and Barr borrowed Nancy's little sports car, the one she gaily called her "fun car," to drive to the feed lot. The cattle-fattening lot was located out of town, and the aroma of several thousand head of cattle was pungent. Niles' second-story, air-conditioned office overlooking the pens of sleek cattle was as elegant and unscented as any downtown businessman's office, however. The occasional sounds of cattle bawling, and a collection of branding irons above Niles' desk lent a note of individuality to the office, but the soft music on the sound system was as quietly conventional as that in any dentist's office.

The two men did go over some figures, and Barr made a point of looking to Vickie for corroboration on some of them, but she had the feeling her presence was hardly essential. Not all the feed-lot cattle came from the Chandler ranch in New Mexico, she learned; some were purchased to make the operation larger and more economical. A computerized system monitored feed mixtures, adjusting them for nutrition and cost. Niles usually ran the operation from the office, but Vickie had the impression that he could personally step in and handle the cattle as expertly as any cowboy if the need arose. The Chandler men were versatile and competent.

Niles took them to lunch at a stockmen's café near the feed lot. It was noisy and unpretentious, but the food was delicious. In spite of her large breakfast, Vickie's appetite was hearty. Barr teased her lightly about being a "growing girl" if she kept eating like that, but his glance at her trim figure was appreciative.

After lunch, Niles closed the office, and they all went to his and Serena's home. It, too, was large and sprawling, with generous space for house guests. Serena said she had some shopping to do and invited Vickie to come along.

Vickie felt a little awkward. Everyone treated her as friend and guest rather than minor employee. She glanced cautiously at Barr for his reaction to the invitation. He didn't look particularly pleased, and Vickie made a small murmur of demurral. Perhaps the business discussion was supposed to continue at the house this afternoon.

Serena caught the exchanged glances between Vickie and Barr and quickly dismissed them. "Don't worry, big brother," she soothed teasingly. "I'll have your pretty lady back in plenty of time for the dinner party tonight. You men can amuse yourselves with Niles' new video game in the den while we're gone."

Your pretty lady. Vickie felt flustered at the way Serena seemed to assume that she was something more than Barr's secretary. Was she? Her heart fluttered in her chest as she looked at him, breath held. She was in love with him—so much in love! Sometimes she could almost believe that her feelings were returned. But nothing could come of it—nothing! All these warm and friendly people would hate her eventually, Barr most of all, because he would feel most personally deceived and betrayed.

No, no, just for this weekend she wouldn't think of that. Just for this weekend she would pretend the future was bright. She gave Barr an arch look, and he finally grinned back, nodding his assent to Serena's invitation.

Serena and Vickie went to a big covered shopping mall, air conditioned, of course. Vickie had planned to wear to the dinner party the same sandals she had on, but she impulsively bought a glamorous pair of heels. Serena had just enrolled in an oil-painting class and was buying supplies. It was a thoroughly enjoyable afternoon.

Barr and Niles were in the pool when Vickie and Serena returned to the house. They joined the men in the pool for a swim and then separated to prepare for the evening out. Barr's room was a couple of doors down from Vickie's lovely, peach-tinted room.

Vickie slipped on the jade dress that had been purchased before she left Shreveport at what seemed an exorbitant price at the time. The cool, filmy material whispered in lush folds around her slim body. The color brought out a green-gold fire in her eyes, and the halter neckline exposed honey and cream shoulders. It also, she realized in dismay, exposed her bra straps, and she had neglected to bring the special bra the dress required.

She had nothing else dressy to wear, so she had no choice but to go without the bra. She removed it and uneasily eyed her reflection in the mirror. Did the lack show? She had high, firm breasts, and the pale jade fabric was opaque, but there seemed a certain lush voluptuousness about her curves in their unfettered state, and the filmy material felt disturbingly sensuous against her bare nipples.

She didn't intend to make a dramatic entrance when she went out to the living room, but that was the way it turned out. Three sets of eyes were suddenly riveted on her as all action and conversation halted.

"You look absolutely gorgeous," Serena declared.

"Like a jade princess," Barr murmured. There was a strange, almost spiritual light in his eyes as they met hers. Then his gaze dropped to the honey-gold shadow between her breasts, and a hint of a distinctly earthy and decidedly nonspiritual hunger flickered across his face.

Vickie felt a moment of outraged indignation. Barr was looking at her as if he might ravish her on the spot, and the look certainly did not escape Serena's interested attention. But Vickie's next reckless thought was that the dress was worth every cent it cost to bring an expression like that to Barr's face! Barr was wearing a black dinner jacket, and with his rangy cowboy build and deep tan the effect was devastatingly attractive, a combination of sophistication and powerful basic masculinity that sent a shivery tingle through Vickie.

They drove to the dinner party in Niles' sleek Lincoln, Barr and Vickie settled in intimate luxury in the back seat. Big, rambling houses seemed almost the norm here, and their host's home was no exception. It was built just under the brow of a boulder-dotted ridge overlooking the city, where lights glimmered like fallen stars in the soft dusk.

At any other time, Vickie might have felt uncomfortable as something of a tag-along guest, but tonight those feelings were lost in her overwhelming relief that there was not going to be a panicky phone call from Benji and Susan's baby sitter to interrupt the festivities. Tonight she was free! No apprehensions, no worries, no duties. Free to enjoy herself. The giddy, bubbly feeling that had simmered within her all day threatened to boil over in sheer exuberance now. She was high on feelings that needed no assistance from the free-flowing champagne. Even when she tried to assume a cool, reserved poise, her smile had a coquettish tilt and her eyes a flirtatious dance that attracted men like a magnet.

Dinner was buffet style. Vickie filled her plate generously. Barr stuck right with her, as if he suspected that some other man might swoop in and make off with her, an action several of the men indeed seemed to have under consideration.

There was dancing after dinner, and Vickie was a little astonished to find that she was the center of male attention. She knew she felt marvelous, but what she didn't know was that she was almost irresistibly desirable in this gay, reckless mood. Barr swept her away before any other man could claim her for a dance, whirling her out on the glass-enclosed balcony overlooking the distant city.

"You're the most beautiful woman here tonight . . . and you know it!" he growled into her ear. He sounded as if he were undecided whether to be proud or resentful.

"I'm just enjoying myself," Vickie answered innocently. She touched the finger tips of her left hand to the crisp chestnut curls at the nape of his neck, a certain sensuous intimacy in the caress that belied the innocence of her voice.

Barr groaned. "You drive me crazy, do you know that? You drive me crazy when you're cool and aloof, the way you've been all week. You drive me even more crazy when you're the way you are tonight!"

"My, you do have a problem, don't you?" She tilted her head back to look up into his glowering eyes, her own innocently wide.

"Yes, I do," he muttered, crushing her to him so closely that she knew he must recognize her braless state now, if he hadn't before. "And that problem is *you.*"

When the music stopped, he whisked her into a secluded corner of the balcony sheltered by greenery, and his hands slipped down to press her body intimately against the hard outline of his. Breathlessly, she lifted her mouth for his kiss, as a voice floated out from the interior of the house.

"Barr, are you out there? Hank wants to ask you about investing in some New Mexico farm land."

Barr, scowling, groaned again and settled for an unsatisfactory peck on the lips. "You just wait," he warned. Vickie shivered lightly as she remembered his earlier warning that there wouldn't always be someone around to interrupt.

On the drive home, Serena snuggled romantically close to Niles on the front seat. Barr did no more than put his arm around Vickie, but the grip was almost fiercely possessive, and she had the feeling that the time of reckoning was at hand, that the sparkling evening had been a mere prelude to something more important —and dangerous. All day and evening she had been irrepressibly bright and bubbly, flirtatious and teasing, blithely brushing aside Barr's twice-repeated warning that they would not always be interrupted at intimate moments. Now the night stretched ahead, filled with tantalizing possibilities, because Barr's room was only two doors from hers, in an otherwise unoccupied wing of the house. . . .

Niles politely offered a nightcap, but Vickie could see that he and Serena were eager to be alone. Vickie declined the offer, murmuring something about a long day. She said good night and excused herself. Barr did not leave the room with her, but the interval between their departures was a bit short for decorum's sake. He caught up with her just as she was turning toward the door to her room.

Her heart tumbled wildly. In the dim hallway, his smile held a warning flash of wicked recklessness. With a little gasp, she snatched at the doorknob. His hand closed over hers.

"Oh, no, you don't. You've been flaunting yourself at me all day. . . ."

"I have not," Vickie protested indignantly. "I do not 'flaunt' myself!" But her protest lacked conviction because she was well aware that in her jubilant, condemned-prisoner-gets-a-reprieve mood, she had teased and tormented him just a little. A foolish thing to do, she now thought wildly. Why hadn't she shown more restraint?

"Vickie, you're fighting me," he said softly as her hand twisted frantically beneath his on the doorknob. "I want to kiss you."

"A g-good-night kiss?"

"If that's what you want it to be."

Reluctantly, feeling almost as if she were letting go of a life line, she released the doorknob. Barr gathered her in his arms with a tender fire. One hand caressed her bare back with softly searing strokes. The other arm clasped her around the waist with a steel-cable strength shielded by velvet gentleness.

He kissed her, slowly, deliberately, as if he were prolonging each moment of the taste and feel of her mouth. The kiss enveloped her, surrounded her, enchanted her. Rich taste of his mouth and spicy scent of his after-shave lotion. Smooth, strong feel of his lips and sweet invasion of his tongue. Thunder of his heartbeat drumming against her breasts and the echo of her own blood pounding in her ears.

When he finally lifted his mouth from hers, his lips touched her closed eyelids lightly. "That didn't feel like a good-night kiss," he said softly. "It felt like a beginning, not an end."

The door to her room stood open in invitation. Had he opened it or had she? Or had it swung open by itself, propelled by some metaphysical force of their combined desires?

He picked her up and carried her into the room, a swift motion of his foot skidding the door shut behind them.

"You can't come in here! What will Niles and Serena think?" Her voice was panicky, but she made no struggle in his arms. Her body felt deliciously languid, suffused with an intoxicating warmth.

He deposited her on the bed and laughed softly. "I rather imagine Niles and Serena are too busy to wonder what you and I are doing. Don't depend on them to chaperone you now, little wildcat! There'll be no more interruptions this night."

"I—I could always say *no* again!"

"Will you?" As he asked the question, he deftly slipped the high-heeled sandals from her feet, his hand taking a leisurely return route over a long nylon-clad leg and hip to return to her waist.

"I don't know!" she said desperately.

He stretched out beside her on the bed, cradling her head against his shoulder. The room was dark except for a dim glow of outdoor lights sifting through the drapes. Against the dark bedspread, her dress was a pale froth crossed by the dark, possessive bands of his arm and leg thrown over her.

"I've missed you, Vickie," he said softly. His finger tips traced the inner curve of her breast, full and lush against the filmy material as she lay on her side.

"But I haven't been gone," she protested. "How could you miss me?"

"I've missed you every night you weren't beside me in my bed with my arms around you." His mouth tantalized the corner of her lips in little exploratory nibbles.

No more than I've missed you, she echoed silently, remembering nights of restless yearning. How could just one night together make every night alone so achingly empty? But what she said was "Why did you bring me along on this trip? You didn't need me to discuss business figures with Niles."

"You figured that out, did you?" His voice held a rich, lazy amusement. "But what else could I say? I had to order you to come. If I'd just invited you, you'd have run like a scared rabbit."

"One moment you tell me I'm a wildcat and the next that I'm a scared rabbit!"

"See? That's what you do to me," he whispered into her ear. His tongue did wild, tantalizing things to her ear lobe. "You make me so mixed up I can't even think straight."

"You've never been mixed up in your life," Vickie accused. "You always know exactly what you're doing."

And what he was doing now was sending tingling messages of desire from his body to hers. She could feel them in the feathery, electric touch of his finger tips, in the warm nuzzle of his lips and the solid pressure of his aroused male body. And her body answered the unvoiced messages as if it had a reckless will of its own disconnected from control of her rational mind. While her mind was saying sensible things like No! Stop this before it goes too far to turn back, her body was straining into even more intimate contact with his, her mouth chasing his fleeting kisses for full contact.

"Do I always know exactly what I'm doing?" He sounded oddly reflective, even as the assault against her senses continued. "I once thought so. But now I wonder. . . ."

His finger tips caressed the exposed inner curve of her breast, the sensitive rosy tip still concealed in the veil of fabric. Then with a small, impatient nudge of his hand, he pushed the material aside and exposed the breast, its delicate skin faintly luminous in the shadows.

"Ah, I thought so," he murmured. He sounded satisfied, as if something he suspected had just been confirmed.

"You thought—what?"

"That you weren't wearing anything underneath." He drew circles around the breast, smaller and smaller until his fingers caressed the nipple to a rigid peak. "Just another of your ways of driving me crazy wanting you."

"But it wasn't deliberate!" Vickie protested. "It was just because I forgot to bring along something proper to wear underneath. . . ."

"You 'forgot.'" He laughed softly, as if he believed that her subconscious had deliberately blotted out all thoughts of bringing along the missing undergarment. He dipped his head to take her breast into his mouth, and the tingling, shooting desires within Vickie coalesced into one all-enveloping blaze. She felt incandescent.

"Vickie, Vickie . . ." Barr groaned, pressing his damp forehead against her breasts. "You drive me wild with wanting you! You can't make me believe you don't want me, too."

I want you, Vickie thought. I love you! But she couldn't make love with him—she couldn't! She'd fought this battle with herself before, knowing that if she gave in to desire, she risked revelation of all she must keep secret.

He caressed the rounded curve of her hip with long, gliding strokes, the touch sensuous but impatient with the barrier of nylon panty hose. She caught his hand as the finger tips slid beneath the band of elastic at her waist.

"No. . . ."

"Vickie, I want to make love with you. Don't tell me—and yourself!—no again."

"I can't. . . ." But even as she said the words, Vickie felt the rebellion of her body gathering against the restraint of her mind, an insurrection that threatened to take control and sweep her along in its growing power.

"Why, Vickie, *why?*" He sounded almost desperate. He covered her face and throat and shoulders and breasts with tender, haunting kisses that she would remember until she died.

"Because I just *can't!*" She shook her head, but her body eagerly arched to meet his caresses, contradicting the rejection of her words. She should never have given in to that first melting kiss at the door, should never have let him into the room. The dangers of future heartbreak were a minor deterrent to her wild desires now, but duty and responsibility still bound her. Even though she loved him, she couldn't run the risk of letting him discover why she had come to the ranch.

And then, from somewhere deep in her subconscious, came the thought that perhaps she could tell him a *part* of the truth and still not give away everything. She could tell him that she had fibbed about being married before, but only because she thought he'd be more likely to hire her if she assured him she was no husband hunter. She could tell him just enough to prevent his asking the otherwise inevitable, surprised questions about her virginity when they made love. And just for now she would close her mind to the heartbreak looming out there in the future.

"Barr . . ." She twisted in his arms, struggling to push herself into an upright position so she could talk to him without the intoxicating distraction of his kisses and caresses. "I have to talk to you, to explain. . . ."

He lifted his mouth from her breasts. "To explain why you're going to say *no* again?" His voice was rough with desire but tinged with a hint of wryness, as if this action were not totally unexpected.

"To tell you that I haven't been entirely honest with you. . . ."

She felt a subtle change in him, a certain wary tightening that reminded her that he could be harshly ruthless as well as tenderly loving. "In what way?" he asked. His voice sounded tautly balanced, as if it could tip toward love or anger.

"I—I told you I'd been married before. . . ."

"Vickie, I don't hold that against you, if that's what is worrying you. Everyone makes mistakes." He brushed his hand over her face, smoothing the disheveled tangle of hair from her temple and cheek. "I just don't think you should punish *me* for the wrongs some other man did you. We don't all cheat or beat our wives or whatever it was he did to you." He kissed her on the tip of the nose.

"No, no—it isn't that. . . ."

"Then what? Just how haven't you been 'entirely honest' with me? You *are* divorced from him, aren't you?" he suddenly asked sharply.

"Yes . . . no. . . ." It wasn't a question that could be

answered yes or no because there never had been a marriage to require a divorce! She took a tremulous breath. "What I mean is, I let you think there was a very bad marriage in my past, that I was cynical about men and love. . . ."

"But you aren't, Vickie," he whispered. "I can feel it in the way you respond to me. No matter what happened in the past, you're too vital and alive not to love again." He dipped his mouth to her breasts again, and a shudder of sweet longing quivered through her.

She tried to protest again, but the words were submerged somewhere inside her as he trailed a ring of delicately fiery kisses around each breast and then moved back to her mouth.

"Vickie, sweetheart, you don't have to tell me some painful secret," he murmured with a soft, sweet huskiness. "Nothing you could say would make me feel any differently about you than I do."

Wouldn't it? she thought wildly. Oh, he was making this so incredibly, painfully difficult!

"No, I have to tell you!" She gasped out the words in a frantic rush before they could get lost again in the delight of his caresses. "There *wasn't* any bad marriage, and I *don't* have some fear of love. . . ."

"You're telling me you're still in love with him? That's the reason you—"

"No!"

But her denial was lost in his fury. "Oh, that explains so much, doesn't it, little wildcat?" He lifted himself up on one elbow to look down at her, and even in the shadowy light she could see the grim twist of his mouth. "You lead me on just far enough to drive me wild, and then you say no because you're still in love with him!"

"No!" Vickie swallowed, gathering her reserves. She was obviously bungling this delicate explanation. He was angry now. And then she felt a surge of answering anger at the way he had misinterpreted what she was trying to say and jumped to the wrong conclusions. Accusing her of leading him on! But at least he had momentarily halted the mind-spinning kisses and caresses so she could think more clearly and get her explanation out.

But before she could say anything, his hold on her tightened, and his hard frame pinned her to the bed. "It doesn't matter," he said roughly. "It doesn't change my feelings. Vickie, I can make you forget him. . . ."

His mouth clamped down on hers with a fierce possessiveness. Gone was the sweet tenderness. The caresses, which had ranged from provocative and seductive to playfully teasing, changed. His aim was to conquer her now, to overwhelm her resistance in a sweeping blaze of passion.

The kiss was deep and probing, a demand for surrender as his tongue invaded her mouth. He ripped off his shirt, and his naked chest met her breasts. His hands slid beneath her body, and relentlessly found their way to bare, silken skin. He molded her body against the harshly male contours of his, granite solid, yet throbbing with life.

She fought back, fought him, fought herself. "Barr, stop. . . ."

She writhed beneath him, but even as she demanded that Barr end his fiery assault, she was caught up in her own passion. It swept through her like a fire storm. It flamed through the last shreds of her resistance and burned away the need for awkward explanations.

She loved him. She wanted to give herself to him—to take him in return! At this moment, that was all that mattered.

He felt her resistance change to submission and the

submission change to an ardent meeting and sharing of his passion.

She tangled her hands in his hair and sought his mouth with her own. She stopped trying to hold herself away from the intimate contact of his body and pressed herself passionately against him.

With Vickie willing and eager in his arms, his harsh aggression softened to a sweet urgency. He unzipped her dress and she slid out of it, uncaring that it fell in a tousled heap on the floor. He stroked her slim body possessively, as if claiming every inch as his own.

"My beautiful little wildcat," he murmured softly. "Tame and purring as a kitten now." He took her hand in his, brushed her finger tips over his jaw and then kissed each one as if it were infinitely precious. "Not a claw in sight."

Kitten. Even as his lips tantalized her finger tips, the word, the name by which she had once been known, jarred Vickie with an intrusion of unwanted thoughts. "Not a kitten," she denied fiercely. "Or a wildcat. Just a woman."

"Oh, yes, every inch a woman," he agreed. He ran a hand from throat to hip over the soft curves that left no doubt about what she was. "The most beautiful, exciting, challenging woman I've ever known."

Challenging. Another jolting word. "Is that how you see me?" she asked uneasily. "As a challenge?"

"Not anymore." His husky chuckle was warm and intimate and his touch confidently proprietary. "A challenge conquered," he whispered as his finger tips sought a new and deeper intimacy.

The awful truth hit her. She was in love with him, but to him she was just a challenge that could not be ignored. He had wanted to prove that *he* was man enough to break through her resistance to men and love! Tonight she had challenged his arrogant male ego even further when he thought she resisted him because she was still in love with someone else. He was ruthlessly determined to prove his own male invincibility, prove that he could make her forget that other lover!

Now he thought victory was imminent. He smugly thought he had conquered her with his expert, passionate lovemaking!

He *had* conquered her, one part of her agreed helplessly. She was in love with him!

But he was not in love with her. She was just a challenge met and vanquished.

Not quite vanquished, she corrected with bitter defiance. This was a victory he had counted too soon.

He had half turned away from her, his hand on his belt buckle, and she used the moment to roll lithely away from him. She swiftly put a chair between them.

"Please go now," she said flatly.

He rolled slowly to a sitting position and then rose to full height beside the bed. There was menace in the taut stance. "Now what?"

"I don't believe I care to be just another victory chalked up to satisfy your male ego. Do you give yourself extra points for conquering a woman who shows an exceptional degree of resistance to your charms?" Vickie had no difficulty keeping her voice scathingly aloof even though the wildfire he had ignited within her still raged.

"You're still in love with him, aren't you?" he accused harshly. "And you'll use any damned argument you can think of to—" He didn't bother to complete the angry accusation. He snatched up his shirt where he had flung it beside her fallen dress and stalked to the door.

"Sweet dreams, little wildcat," he said grimly. "May dreams and memories of your old love be enough to keep you company in your cold bed."

No! she cried silently. Sweet dreams were not enough. And the only memories she had that mattered were of *him*.

Chapter Eight

The atmosphere in the plane on the flight from Phoenix to the ranch late Sunday afternoon was so tense and brittle that it seemed about to shatter. Or perhaps, thought Vickie tautly, it was just *she* who was about to shatter.

Barr concentrated with a raw determination on flying the plane, a set, uncompromising expression on his face. *He* would never shatter, Vickie thought. Conflict between love and duty would never tear *him* apart. Mrs. Chandler acted vaguely troubled, as if she knew something was wrong but didn't know what it was. Even the children were subdued.

Ric was waiting at the airstrip with a car when the plane landed. Barr said brusquely that he had some things to do with the plane and told Ric to return for him later. On the short drive to the house, the children's usual liveliness returned, and they chattered animatedly with their father about the weekend events.

Vickie felt as exhausted as if she had spent the weekend digging ditches and lugging rocks—activities, she thought wryly, that would probably have been more productive than what she *had* done this disastrous weekend.

Over the next week, Vickie kept telling herself that Barr's jumping to the wrong conclusion was really quite fortunate for her. Otherwise, she might not have realized until too late the real reason behind his determination to make love to her—a reason, she thought bleakly, that was far different from her reason for wanting to make love with him. Yes, it was better this way. Now she could simply get on with what she had to do here.

Yet she couldn't really convince herself that she was "fortunate" or that things were "better." She certainly didn't *feel* fortunate. She felt miserable and mixed up, awkward and uneasy when she was in Barr's presence, lonely and unhappy when she was out of it.

Each night, as she lay in her bed alone, she battled an almost overpowering urge to toss caution and pride and logic to the winds, go brazenly to his room and throw herself at him. She conquered the urge, but she was suspicious of her traitorous subconscious, half afraid that she would sometime waken and find that she had walked in her sleep and acted out her wild desires.

The ranch was busy now. Barr was culling the herds, weeding out the cattle that were not worth carrying through the winter. His hours in the office were irregular, but Vickie was uncertain whether this was because of the press of outside duties or his hostility toward her. He was elaborately careful to avoid any physical contact between them. There was not even an accidental brushing of hands or touch of shoulders in passing. Sometimes she felt his eyes on her, but whenever she dared sneak a glance at him, he appeared engrossed in his work, and she knew she must merely be indulging in a bit of wishful thinking.

All activity on the ranch, it appeared, would come to a temporary halt over the Labor Day weekend when

Amanda's Baby was scheduled to run in the million-dollar All-American Futurity at Ruidoso Downs. Even most of the ranch hands were planning to go down for the race and cheer the ranch favorite on.

Vickie had not called Kathy since the weekend in Phoenix. Part of the reason was that she really hadn't anything to tell Kathy until she could ascertain whether or not the race weekend held any possibilities for snatching the children. The other part of the reason Vickie hadn't called was less concrete. She hadn't lost any of her feeling that she *owed* Kathy and Aunt Verla all the help she could give them. She was infuriated anew with Ric each time she thought about his telling the children that their mother was dead. She knew Kathy missed the children desperately. But she couldn't help wondering if Kathy, after she got the children back, would hide them off somewhere where their father couldn't see them—and where the children couldn't see him, either, of course. Somehow, no matter what happened, it seemed to Vickie that the children themselves were going to be shortchanged.

The weekend limped by. The days were exceptionally hot, and Vickie lazed around the pool. On Saturday, Barr and Ric went into Albuquerque and returned with two new pickups for the ranch. On Sunday, Mrs. Chandler gave a buffet dinner for members of one of her charity committees. The committee members appeared to have an extraordinarily large number of marriageable daughters, most of whom, Vickie suspected, had come along for the sole purpose of making contact with Barr. That ought to soothe his bruised ego, Vickie thought sourly as she watched the girls vie for the privilege of flirting with him.

Barr, however, evidently didn't find the eager girls enough of a challenge. His stay at the buffet lasted only long enough to avoid outright rudeness. He made even less of an attempt to be polite to Vickie, ignoring her completely.

He was absent from the office all day Monday but finally stalked in after lunch on Tuesday. Vickie's nervous reaction only moments later was accidentally to nudge her coffee cup off the edge of the desk. She was down on her knees on the floor wiping up the broken glass and coffee when the phone rang.

Barr gave her a hooded look. "I'll get it," he muttered.

Vicki grimaced as she threw the soggy, stained paper towel into a wastepaper basket. She had just started toward the door, intending to dampen another towel in the nearby bathroom and pick up the remaining shards of glass, when Barr called her back.

"It's for you," he said. "A man." His voice was flat, yet somehow faintly contemptuous.

Vickie picked up the phone at her desk, more puzzled than apprehensive. What man could possibly be calling her here? Unless it was the printer's office, returning her call about changing the letterhead on the ranch stationery. She said a brisk hello.

"Vickie?" The unfamiliar male voice sounded guarded. "Kathy wants to talk to you."

"Kitten, I know I shouldn't have called you, but it's been so long since I've heard anything that I was just about to go crazy!"

Kitten. The name was a jarring reminder of Barr's teasing wildcat-kitten murmurs. "Please don't call me that!" she snapped nervously, totally rattled by hearing Kathy's voice with Barr looking on. Out of the corner of her eye she could see that Barr was not making even a polite pretense of not listening to her end of the conversation.

"Call you what?" Kathy sounded bewildered.

"What you—always call me. Oh, skip it! It doesn't matter." She drew a steadying breath. "I'm sorry I haven't called you, but there just wasn't any reason to call."

"It's difficult for you to talk? Someone is with you? Barr?" Kathy guessed.

"Yes, that's right."

"That's why I had Al place the call," Kathy explained. Al was the hired expert who was supposed to help her get the kids back. "We figured if someone other than you answered the phone, whoever it was would think a male caller asking for you was just a boy friend."

"Possibly."

"You can let Barr think it's that ex-husband you told him you had," Kathy said with a laugh. "I'll try to phrase my questions so you can answer without giving away that you're talking to me instead of your 'ex.' Okay?"

Vickie suspected that Barr already thought she was talking to her "ex-husband." His expression was metallic, as rigid as the sculptured bronze cowboy on the shelf behind him. Kathy didn't know how much she was asking, Vickie thought despairingly. Vickie didn't *want* Barr to think she was talking to an old lover. Yet at the moment she had no other choice.

"First, are the kids okay?" Kathy asked.

"Yes. Fine."

"Did anyone remember Benji's birthday?"

"Yes. Very nicely."

"Are there any activities or dates coming up in the near future when the kids will be off the ranch and we might be able to get them?" Kathy went on.

"Possibly."

"But you can't say when?"

"In the fairly near future. I'll have to call you."

Vickie felt rivulets of nervous perspiration trickle down her skin.

"Kitten—I mean Vickie, you sound upset."

"It's just that this is—is very difficult for me." Vickie ran a tissue over her damp throat. Her blouse felt plastered to her back. The strain of trying to phrase answers to Kathy's questions so that Barr would still think she was talking to her "ex-husband" was excruciating.

"I'm sorry. I know I shouldn't have called," Kathy said, repeating her earlier apology. "It's just that I get so worried. And sometimes I *do* get the feeling that you're falling for Barr, and that makes me wonder if you might change your mind and not call me."

"No!" The word came out sharper than Vickie intended. "That's ridiculous. Please don't worry about that. I gave you my word." Grimly, she hoped Kathy wouldn't notice that she had not, however, denied the accusation about falling for Barr.

"Okay, hon. I'll try to be patient and just wait for you to call," Kathy promised.

"Yes, I'd prefer to call you."

Vickie replaced the phone, surreptitiously wiped her damp hands on the already ragged tissue and instantly resumed her typing.

She jumped when Barr spoke, his voice coming from a point just over her right shoulder. So intent was she on appearing busy and normal that she hadn't even heard his approach.

"Your speed is admirable." His tone was mocking as he looked down at the letter she was typing. "Too bad not as much may be said for your accuracy."

Vickie looked at what she had typed. Her fingers had been on the wrong keys and one entire line of the letter was an incomprehensible jumble. She snatched the paper out of the machine.

"Does he call you often?" Barr inquired.

"No."

"Usually, you call him."

"I'm sorry the personal call came during working hours." Vickie rolled another sheet of paper into the typewriter, realized that she had forgotten carbon paper and second sheet and rolled the single paper out again with trembling fingers. Her ruse on the phone had obviously been one hundred percent effective. Barr thought the caller was her "ex-husband." He was watching her discomfort and nervousness with undisguised scorn. "I'll put in extra time to make up for the time lost, of course," she muttered.

"That won't be necessary. You're most conscientious about putting in more than enough time on office work." He made the fact sound like a liability rather than an asset.

Vickie noted the shards of her broken coffee cup still littering the floor by her desk. She was not, however, about to get down on her hands and knees to pick them up while Barr stood over her like a denim-clad inquisitor.

"I hadn't realized until now that you were still in contact with your ex-husband," Barr said grimly. "But then, I also hadn't realized until rather recently that you're still in love with him."

The words came out a malicious taunt, as if he challenged her to deny them. And deny them she could not! She felt as if she were trapped in some gigantic web. Now she couldn't even tell Barr no ex-husband existed, that she had fibbed simply to get the job, because that would leave her in the position of having to explain the male caller on the phone. Lies and more lies . . .

"I really believe my personal affairs are no concern of yours." Vickie tried to maintain an aloof dignity, but dignity was difficult when her recalcitrant fingers persisted in typing nonsense on the page.

"Perhaps not. But when your personal affairs start affecting your job performance, perhaps I do have a right to be concerned." He put a certain mocking emphasis on the word *affairs,* giving it the worst connotation possible. His hand moved over the typewriter, stilling her frantically racing fingers. "He has a powerful effect on you. You're trembling."

The "he" who didn't exist had no effect on her at all. But Barr himself did. She was aware to the core of her being of the strength in the hand covering hers, the first time he had touched her since Phoenix. His denim-clad thigh was only inches away, and she fought an impossible impulse to wrap her hands around it and press her cheek to the hard muscles. She felt his other hand go to the back of her neck, the grasp a harsh bite into her flesh.

"What does he call you?" Barr demanded abruptly.

"Call me?" Vickie repeated blankly.

"You told him on the phone not to call you by some specific name." His finger tips dug into the nape of her neck as if he were tempted to pick her up and shake her. "What was it? And what's supposed to happen in the near future with him?"

"How dare you listen to my private conversation and then—then interrogate me about it!" Vickie gasped in outrage.

"I told you, when personal matters interfere with job performance—"

"It's not my job performance you're concerned about," Vickie snapped. "It's my bedroom performance. Or lack thereof. Because your arrogant male pride won't let you admit that some woman might be impervious to your expert lovemaking."

His hand dropped from her neck as if he had been

electrically shocked. She had the small satisfaction of seeing that she had at least jarred that carved, expressionless mask off his face. His sage-green eyes flashed surprise, and he had to make an effort to clamp his jaw shut. She could almost believe that the sun-browned skin flushed slightly. Obviously, he had not expected such a blunt, outspoken reaction from her.

Barr stalked back to his desk, and Vickie tasted a small but sweet victory.

The taste was painfully brief.

The beginning sequence of the next few minutes' events was a rerun of what had happened only moments earlier. Vickie was cleaning up the last bits of broken glass. The phone rang. Barr muttered that he'd get it.

For a moment, Vickie had the feeling that time had stalled and that she must go through the entire impossible scene again. But the feeling ended with Barr's next words.

"Lou Ann!" He spoke the name loudly and with warm enthusiasm. "How nice to hear from you."

They chatted for several minutes. Barr told Lou Ann about the Phoenix trip—though he did omit a few intimate details, Vickie noted wryly. Determined to ignore the conversation, Vickie returned to her typing, only to have Barr hold his hand over the phone and request that she hold off the typing for a few minutes. The noise was interrupting his phone conversation, he stated.

"Sorry," Vickie mumbled. Evidently, this call was more important than his mere *business* calls, because the sound of the typewriter never bothered him then.

He returned to the phone. "What was that you were saying, Lou Ann? The barbecue is when?"

With eyes fixed on Vickie, Barr made a date with Lou Ann for Saturday afternoon and evening, spelling out the details clearly. Vickie could almost suspect that the deliberate repetition of details was for her benefit. Just as deliberately, she made a point of walking out on the conversation. That move was no victory, however. It was retreat, pure and simple. Hearing him talk and laugh with Lou Ann filled her with frustrated rage and numbing pain.

Just in case Vickie had missed any details, Barr spelled them out again at dinner that evening. Mrs. Chandler's eyebrows lifted, and she shot Vickie a surprised glance, but her murmur was noncommittal.

Vickie purposely went for a horseback ride on Saturday afternoon and was not around to see Barr leave for his date with Lou Ann. There was one small detail about the barbecue that Barr didn't know. After Barr's call from Lou Ann, Hale Wardlow had telephoned and invited Vickie to attend the same event, but she had politely declined. There would have been a certain satisfaction in surprising Barr by showing up at the barbecue and dance, but not enough satisfaction to neutralize the pain of watching Barr and Lou Ann together. Lou Ann would, no doubt, also be going down to the big race at Ruidoso next weekend, which was another disheartening thought.

Vickie was under the impression that the children would not be going to Ruidoso, but she couldn't be certain. She was keeping under consideration the thought that if Benji and Susan were left on the ranch with only a skeleton crew around, it might be possible to snatch them directly from the ranch.

Excitement over the race was building day by day. Mrs. Chandler was like a child expectantly awaiting Christmas. She was on the phone almost daily, anxiously checking on the filly's condition. Vickie knew that the enormous amount of money involved in the race was important, but it was not Mrs. Chandler's primary interest. The filly truly was her "baby," and she was as concerned and nervous as any proud mother. The Albuquerque newspaper ran an article, with pictures, about the filly, and one photo showed a scrawny, month-old filly sucking on a bottle held by Mrs. Chandler. At this point, with the race just a few days away, almost everyone agreed that Amanda's Baby had the speed to run away from her competition, but she was still not favored to win the race. She had been plagued with bad luck, from the initial death of her dam to various minor ailments and injuries, and race-track followers were aware that bad luck could nullify speed and strength.

The ranch was quiet when Vickie rode into the yard and unsaddled her horse. The air smelled dry and dusty. In spite of the late-summer heat, there was already an undertone of autumn in the air. Vickie loved the fall season, but sometimes it made her feel a little sad. Fall was a time of endings, and she was heavily conscious of an end inexorably closing in on her even though she was not yet certain of the exact date and time. As Vickie neared the house, she heard the familiar sounds of the children playing around the pool.

Inside, she started down the hallway toward her room, then caught her breath as she saw a lanky silhouette at the far end of the hall. Hadn't Barr gone to the barbecue with Lou Ann, after all?

Then the figure moved, and with disappointment Vickie realized that it wasn't Barr, after all. It was only Ric. Just then a childish shriek echoed down the hallway.

"Daddy! Daddy! Grandma hurt herself!"

Ric instantly disappeared around the end of the hallway, and Vickie took a racing shortcut to the pool through the side door. Mrs. Chandler lay beside the pool, legs drawn up in pain. Ric was bending over her.

"What happened?" Vickie gasped.

Mrs. Chandler grimaced. "A clumsy old lady tried to catch a Frisbee and fell flat on her tail bone." She tried to sit up. "I'll be all right. Just help me to my room."

Vickie and Ric exchanged glances. Mrs. Chandler was not all right. Her usually healthy tan looked blotchy and sallow over the pale skin underneath. She had a fist pressed into the small of her back as if trying to block the pain from there.

"I think she'd better go to the hospital," Vickie said firmly.

Ric nodded. Mrs. Chandler grumbled, but she was in too much pain to protest very effectively. Ric rigged up a makeshift stretcher with a board and blanket, and together he and Vickie carried Mrs. Chandler to the car. Benji and Susan stood around looking scared and wide-eyed.

Vickie tucked a blanket around Mrs. Chandler in the car.

Mrs. Chandler was still wearing her swim suit, since changing clothes in her injured condition had not seemed advisable. Vickie patted the older woman's arm reassuringly, but she was very much aware of Mrs. Chandler's earlier, serious back injury.

"Vickie, would you take the children over to Carol?" Mrs. Chandler asked, efficiently thinking of details in spite of her pain. "They'll probably keep me in the hospital overnight."

"Carol went to visit her sister this weekend," Ric cut in.

Doñela had also taken the day off. Both Ric and Mrs. Chandler looked questioningly at Vickie, and she hesitated only momentarily before promising that she would look after the children. Mrs. Chandler smiled and squeezed Vickie's hand in thanks, obviously fully confident in her. As Ric was sliding into the driver's seat of the car, he tossed over his shoulder a request that Vickie get hold of Barr and tell him what had happened.

Vickie took the children inside and helped them change out of their swim suits. She telephoned the ranch where the barbecue was being held. Barr couldn't immediately be located, but she left an emergency message for him.

Then she was faced with a dilemma. She had the children now. There was nothing to stop her from loading them into her car and driving off with them. It would be so simple. She could probably be in Amarillo before the Chandlers ever realized that Susan and Benji were missing. Kathy and Aunt Verla would be overjoyed. The golden opportunity had fallen on Vickie like some unexpected gift from heaven. It would be a betrayal of Kathy and Aunt Verla *not* to snatch the opportunity and run with it.

Yet Vickie just couldn't bring herself to do it. Kathy would be furious if she knew, Vickie thought guiltily. She would say that taking the children in this situation was no worse than Ric's stealing the children from Aunt Verla. But Vickie still couldn't do it. It was too sneaky, too underhanded, far worse than simply outwitting the Chandlers to get the children. It would be taking advantage of Mrs. Chandler when she was down and helpless, betraying the temporary trust she had placed in Vickie. A little defiantly, Vickie reminded herself that she had never agreed actually to snatch the children herself. Only to make a phone call.

Vickie was fixing dinner for the children when Barr returned her call. There was music and laughter in the background. Barr listened while Vickie explained what had happened, then said tersely that he would drive to the hospital immediately. Vickie was so concerned about Mrs. Chandler's accident that she couldn't even take any satisfaction in the knowledge that it had played havoc with Barr's and Lou Ann's evening together.

Vickie fed the children and nibbled a few bites herself, but she was too jittery to eat much. Random, disorganized thoughts rattled around in her mind. Perhaps they should have left Mrs. Chandler lying where she was and called an ambulance instead of moving her themselves. Was it really honor that had kept her from running off with the kids at this particular time—or something less admirable that had to do with her feelings for Barr? What if Mrs. Chandler was permanently disabled? Would Lou Ann accompany Barr to the hospital?

The questions were as unanswerable as they were disjointed. Vickie gave Benji and Susan their bedtime baths, read stories until their eyes drooped and then put them to bed, reassuring Benji that grandma's fall was not his fault just because he had thrown the Frisbee. Susan unexpectedly gave Vickie a big sleepy hug, a sweetly affectionate gesture that left Vickie with a fresh conflict of emotions. By not taking the children now, when she had the opportunity, she was denying Kathy the warm, wonderful feel of her children's hugs. . . .

Two cars drove into the ranch yard at about midnight. Vickie was still restlessly watching television in the den. She went out to meet Barr and Ric. Both men looked weary. Barr's white dress shirt was partly unbuttoned, and his hair looked as if he had dragged his fingers through it numerous times.

Vickie's first thought—of which she was instantly ashamed—was that Barr evidently had not taken Lou Ann to the hospital with him. Quickly, she asked the question that was far more important. "How is your mother?"

"There's nothing broken. Actually, it's primarily

aggravation of the old injury she suffered years ago," Barr said. "They gave her pain killers and muscle relaxants tonight. She says we're all making a big fuss over nothing, but she'll be in bed for a while. Perhaps in traction for a few days."

Vickie felt relieved. It was more than the overnight stay Mrs. Chandler had predicted but far less than the total disaster Vickie had feared. "I'm glad it's nothing more serious."

"That depends on your definition of 'serious,'" Barr said somberly. "I rather imagine she's going to consider it damned serious when she finds out she's going to be flat on her back in bed when Amanda's Baby runs next weekend."

Chapter Nine

Mrs. Chandler came home on Thursday, over the grumblings of her doctor, who would have preferred that she remain in the Albuquerque hospital a bit longer. With her came a bulky hospital bed, a complicated-looking traction device and a brisk nurse. By that time, Mrs. Chandler was resigned to the fact that she would have to watch the big race on television rather than in person at the race track.

By now, Vickie also realized just how important the race was. The All-American Futurity was for quarter horses on the level of importance with the Kentucky Derby for thoroughbreds. It was, in fact, the world's richest horse race, with a cool million for the winner and a total purse of some two and a half million dollars.

That evening, Vickie herded the children into their grandmother's room for a good-night kiss. She had been helping care for them while Mrs. Chandler was in the hospital. Barr was with his mother, and the children included him in their generous round of good-night kisses.

"Oh, Vickie," Mrs. Chandler called as Vickie and the children were leaving, "would you come in tomorrow and do a few letters for me? I'd like to get them out before you leave for Ruidoso."

"Of course. But I'm not leaving. . . ."

"You're not?" Mrs. Chandler looked shocked, as if Vickie had made some truly astounding announcement. "But everyone is going."

Vickie felt uncomfortable. She hadn't been included in any of the exciting Labor Day weekend plans. Barr appeared totally absorbed in a spot on the ceiling. "I really don't have any way to go or place to stay. . . ."

"You can fly down with Barr. And stay in the motel room I was supposed to have. We've had rooms reserved in Ruidoso for months. They're impossible to get if you wait until the last minute."

Barr studied the ceiling.

"Thanks, but I don't think—"

"You really must go," Mrs. Chandler said decisively. "Amanda's Baby likes women. You can take a message to her that Amanda loves her." There was a little catch in her throat and an extra brightness in her eyes when she added, "Whether or not she wins."

"You might as well come," Barr muttered. He sounded as if he begrudged even those few skimpy words.

Such enthusiasm for her presence, Vickie stormed silently. If he was deliberately trying to sound indifferent, he certainly succeeded. But she really wanted to see the race, and with a defiant glance at Barr, said as much.

Almost everyone was planning to leave on Friday or Saturday and spend the full holiday weekend at the Ruidoso Downs' races, but Barr said he wasn't flying down until Sunday. The All-American Futurity race was set for Monday, Labor Day itself.

"Sunday afternoon will be fine," Vickie agreed coolly.

The thought gnawed at Vickie that the coming weekend would be a perfect opportunity for Kathy and her hired helper to come right onto the ranch and snatch the children. On the day of the race, only Mrs. Chandler, Doñela and the children would be there. A wide-open opportunity. . . .

Yet, again, berating herself for being softhearted and foolish, Vickie could not bring herself to inflict this added blow on Mrs. Chandler just now. Vickie was also afraid that if Mrs. Chandler was practically alone on the ranch, she might try to get out of bed to prevent the children from being taken and further injure herself. No, the children could not be taken this weekend.

Only Vickie and Barr were in the plane on the flight to Ruidoso Sunday. Barr was silent, with a preoccupied, faintly hostile air. No one met them at the small airport, and they took a cab to the motel.

Located high in the cool, pine-forested Sacramento Mountains, the Ruidoso area was far different from the flat, bare range land around the Chandler ranch. Most of the pleasant but "touristy"-looking town appeared to be strung out along the main highway winding through the green mountains. The houses were mostly steep-roofed chalets rather than the low desert-style houses that Vickie always thought of as typical New Mexican. Barr brusquely said that Ruidoso was a horse-racing town in summer but a ski area in winter.

Barr was sharing a room with Ric; Vickie had a room to herself. The other Chandlers, plus a host of friends, were scattered along the second floor of the motel. Everyone was friendly and welcoming to Vickie, but she was uncomfortably aware that she was here only because Mrs. Chandler had practically forced Barr to bring her. She felt out of place in the festive atmosphere that permeated the whole town in anticipation of the final and most important day of the racing season.

154

There were several lively parties going on in the motel that evening, but Vickie slipped away early and went to her room. She didn't know what had become of Barr in the exuberant crowd. She hadn't yet seen Lou Ann, but she knew that the girl must be around somewhere.

Vickie was by now accustomed to rising early and automatically did so the next morning. She was just getting ready to go downstairs for coffee and Danish when a knock startled her. Barr also looked startled when, fully dressed, she immediately opened the door.

"I take it you didn't stay up until all hours partying like everyone else?" He made the question sound like an accusation, as if he suspected she'd spent the time on the phone with her "ex-husband."

"No." And where were *you?* she wondered, but she didn't ask.

"I'm going out to the track to watch the filly's morning exercise. Do you want to come along?"

Vickie nodded, suspecting, however, that she was invited only because no one else was up yet. They had breakfast in the motel's coffee shop, then went out to the track. The grandstand was empty, of course, but the stable area bustled with activity. Horses whinnied and stomped in their stalls. An automatic walking machine led several steaming horses in a circle to cool them down after a workout. A man on a placid saddle horse led an excited mare that bounced along as if she had springs on her feet. The cool morning air was scented with horseflesh and dust and fresh hay, and excitement hung over the track as palpably as the dust. For the first time, Vickie felt a stirring of that excitement within her.

Amanda's Baby was given a very light workout, just enough to keep her loosened up for the race that afternoon. Everyone affectionately called the filly

"Baby," but Vickie was a little awed by her. She was big and powerful, with sculptured muscles that rippled under her satin-sleek sorrel skin and a lean belly tucked up like a greyhound's. Her nostrils flared as she arched her powerful neck and danced alongside the man leading her back to the stall.

But back in her stall, the nuzzle of her velvety nose against Vickie's hand was friendly, her brown eyes meltingly soft. Vickie tentatively fed her a scrap of hay, and she took it with a dainty, ladylike nibble of soft lips. Then, affectionate as some child's pet, she put her head down, wanting her ears scratched, and Vickie obliged. While Barr talked with the trainer, Vickie even whispered Mrs. Chandler's message, feeling a little foolish but at the same time half suspecting that the sweet-natured filly understood. She truly was a "baby" at heart, if not in powerful appearance or performance.

By the time the Chandler crowd approached the race track that afternoon, the charged atmosphere had heightened. The parking lot and the grandstand with its colored seats seethed with activity. The American flag waved proudly, and music blared. The betting windows were already busy.

The track was a smooth oval with a long straightaway leading into it. A shallow pond glittered within the oval. Barr said that thoroughbreds ran the full oval track, but quarter horses, like Amanda's Baby, raced only the straightaway for their short, explosive bursts of speed. He said there was an old saying that quarter-horse races were so fast that you'd better not blink or you might miss the whole thing. The All-American Futurity was four hundred and forty yards, and the expected racing time something under twenty-two seconds. And a million dollars rested on those few seconds!

Barr was outwardly calm, but a dark glitter in his eyes betrayed his excitement. The others were less controlled, Nancy and Serena bubbling with excitement. Vickie felt a tension growing within her, a mounting desperate hope that Amanda's Baby would win the race. She wanted Mrs. Chandler to have that victory to in some small way counterbalance the loss that was soon coming.

The less important races came first, of course, excitement building toward the million-dollar race that was the high point of the racing season. Vickie bet on some of the races because everyone was doing it, but she scarcely knew if she won or lost. Nancy dropped a winning ticket, disappeared into a jungle of feet to search for it and came up disheveled but victorious.

The last race before the All-American Futurity ended. By that time, dark clouds moved across the sky, getting ready for the summer-afternoon rainstorm that often freshened the mountain air.

And then the moment had come. A new set of figures showing the betting odds on the big race flashed on the board. Something happened in the crowd, a quick leap of excitement, like music jumping an octave higher and increasing in tempo.

The horses were saddled and then paraded around the track, led by the state's governor mounted on a saddle horse. The betting favorite was a big black colt, the gamblers a little leery of Amanda's Baby because of her reputation for bad luck. Vickie thought the black had an evil-natured set to his ears. Amanda's Baby was nervous but not unduly excited. She danced on springy hoofs, a small froth of foam at the corners of her mouth. There was nothing of the "baby" about her here; she looked every inch the magnificent race horse that she was. The odds on her had gone down when

Vickie glanced at the board again. Plenty of people had faith in her ability to run in spite of bad luck!

Oh, please, please, please win, Vickie found herself repeating over and over to herself as she watched the delicately powerful movements of the velvet-eyed filly. Run like you've never run before! Vickie was so wound up in her private litany that she didn't realize Barr had spoken to her until he emphasized the question with a light touch on her arm.

"Are you betting on her?" he asked with a questioning arch of his eyebrows.

Vickie stared at him. Then she shook her head almost violently, her green eyes dark with emotion. No, she wouldn't bet on Amanda's Baby! Not usually superstitious, she suddenly felt that if she bet on Amanda's Baby, the filly wouldn't win. Ridiculous, she knew, but an overpowering feeling nevertheless.

Barr misunderstood. His mouth twisted in a cynical smile. "Thanks for your good wishes and encouraging vote of confidence," he said sarcastically. "We needed that."

"No, it isn't that. . . ."

But he was already gone, threading his way through the crowd to the betting area, ready to back the ranch's pride and joy with hard dollars.

Moments later, the horses were parading to the blue starting gate. They were behind it, then, one by one, in it. Amanda's Baby was in the number-three box. A horse reared and came down with a bruising crash.

Not Baby. Oh, Lord, thank you, Vickie breathed, momentarily squeezing her eyes shut.

The gate burst open, and the field of ten horses exploded onto the track. Sorrels and bays—and a black flash in front! Where are you? Vickie screamed within herself. Where are you? There was little time in a quarter-horse race for a horse to recover from a bad start, no time to slowly inch up on a front runner. It took a blinding flash of speed to win, heart and courage and judgment and more than a little sheer luck.

The horses thundered down the wide track, the screams of people goading them on and a rumble of thunder echoing from the darkening clouds overhead. And then Vickie screamed aloud as she finally spotted the gallant filly, giving every ounce of her big heart, stretching and reaching and surging alongside the big black.

"Run, Baby, run!" Vickie screamed, her voice joining the roar of shouts. "Run!"

The race seemed at the same time unending and over before it had begun. It seemed as if that field of horses had always been out there, sweating and straining and racing their hearts out. And then it was all over, sorrel nose and black together, and Vickie didn't know for certain what had happened until Barr picked her up in his arms and tossed her in the air with a wild whoop of joy.

"She did it! She did it—she won!"

Then the announcer was calling for the owners, and all the Chandlers were streaming toward the flower-bordered winner's circle. They made a crowd of their own: Ric, Niles and Serena, Nancy and Bill, Barr bringing up the rear. And then Barr was pulling Vickie along, too, dragging her with an iron grip on her hand.

Then they were all standing in the winner's circle beside the lathered, hard-breathing horse. A blanket of red, white and blue was draped over her shoulders, and the jockey's grin beautified his angular face. Flash bulbs popped, and everyone hugged everyone else. A television camera was rolling, and someone thrust a microphone in Barr's face. He said how proud they all were of the filly, but the proudest owner of all, Mrs. Chandler, couldn't be here today, and if it weren't for her love and determination, none of this would have happened. Then there was a trophy and a check, an honest-to-God million-dollar check. Vickie was laughing and crying along with the others, not certain why she was doing either but clutching Barr's hand as if her life depended on it.

And then, with a rumble of thunder, the clouds opened up, and everyone was instantly drenched in the downpour. Vickie's hair was plastered wetly to her head, and her eyelashes glittered with raindrops and tears. Her clothes were soaked, and rivulets of water trickled down her back, but none of that mattered because Barr kissed her. Right there in front of the thousands in the grandstand and more thousands watching on television, he kissed her.

Somehow they all made it out of the winner's circle, wet, dripping, laughing. Amanda's Baby, calm now but prancing a little as if she knew she had done something very special, was taken back to the stable area to be properly cooled down, having just raced her way to a million dollars and a place in quarter-horse history.

The small crowd of jubilant Chandlers trooped inside the Turf Club to get out of the wind and the last of the brief but soaking downpour. Barr was still holding tightly to Vickie's hand. Then someone mentioned that this victory deserved a real celebration, and they all looked at each other, knowing no celebration could be complete without their mother present.

Then Barr suggested holding off celebrating until they got back to the ranch, and suddenly a full-blown extravaganza was in the works for the following evening. A big barbecue, music, an open invitation to any- and everyone who wanted to come. The plans expanded by leaps and bounds. And they would haul the star of the show, Amanda's Baby, home for the festivities, too!

Could they do all that on one day's notice? Vickie wondered doubtfully. It sounded like the kind of event that required weeks of planning and arranging. But Vickie hadn't allowed for the Chandlers' fiery spirit and fierce determination when they got going on a project. Duties were delegated, plans made. Nancy exuberantly shouted an invitation to a Stetson-hatted man across the room and got an immediate wave and nod of acceptance.

They were going to make it work, Vickie realized in astonishment. They were going to throw a celebration that would be remembered for years!

There was much to do, not the least of which was cash in the winning betting tickets on Amanda's Baby. Barr went off to call Mrs. Chandler and then make arrangements to have the filly hauled to the ranch. He seemed to have forgotten Vickie, but he had a great many other things to think about, she rationalized. She went back to the motel with Nancy and Serena. No one noticed that she was a little more quiet than the others.

This was it, Vickie realized with a dark sense of doom as she went alone to her room to dry off and change clothes. The time had come. There would be so much confusion and excitement at the ranch, so many people coming and going, that Kathy and her hired helper could boldly come right to the ranch and snatch the kids.

Vickie felt a plunge of dismay, a thud of raw despair. No, not yet. . . .

But she couldn't put it off any longer, couldn't escape it. This was the climax of the mission for which she had come. It was the perfect time. She wasn't hitting the Chandlers when they were down. She could no longer use that excuse. They were winners, million-dollar winners. Kathy would also be a winner with her children back in her arms.

Only Vickie was a loser, a loser forever. . . .

But it was what she had always known was coming, she reminded herself bleakly. She had known she must not fall in love with Barr Chandler—and she had done it, anyway.

Was there consolation in knowing that Barr's feelings for her were something different than the all-encompassing love she felt for him, that he saw her only as a challenge to be conquered?

If there was any consolation there, Vickie had yet to find it. And whatever feelings he did have for her would instantaneously vanish in a volcano of wrath when he realized her devious role on the ranch.

She picked up the phone in her motel room, felt like a traitor and set it down again. These people had been good to her. She didn't want them to hate her—didn't want Barr to hate her! Yet if she didn't place the call, she was betraying Kathy and Aunt Verla, turning her back on her duty and promise.

She was trapped, caught between desire and duty.

No, it went deeper than that. She was torn between two loves: love for the family that had raised and cared for her, love for the man who had taken eternal possession of her heart. No matter what she did, she betrayed someone she loved.

Yet she couldn't just go on like this, squirming helplessly like some wild animal with a foot caught in a trap, because there was Kathy's love to consider, also. Kathy's love for her children and her growing desperation to get them back.

Vickie placed the call. In just a few moments, it was done. The wheels were in motion. There was no turning back now. Kathy and her hired helper would come to the ranch after dark. Vickie would bring the children to them. They would drive away, and then

Vickie would slip into her own car and disappear in the confusion of the celebration.

Vickie hung up the phone feeling drained and a little numb. By tomorrow night, it would be all over. Only the pain of her heartbreak would linger on.

The other Chandlers were packed and ready to leave for the ranch within minutes. They offered Vickie a ride, but she declined. The flight back to the ranch would be her last minutes alone with Barr. It was a sweet torture she had decided to allow herself.

Bare minutes after the others left, Vickie's phone shrilled. It was the horse trainer's assistant with a message from Barr. Amanda's Baby, with her unfortunate penchant for bad luck, had been slightly injured, and Barr was staying overnight in Ruidoso. Vickie could ride back to the ranch with Niles or Nancy. Vickie merely thanked the man and didn't explain that it was too late for that. She felt a pain, a bleakness, a death of hope. Barr was trying to send her away. The kiss at the race had meant nothing. It was just Barr's excited reaction to the victory.

She waited restlessly in her room until after dark and then went down to the restaurant for coffee. When she returned, there was a light on in Barr's room. She hesitated, then walked to his door and knocked briskly.

"Who is it?" his muffled voice called back.

"Vickie."

A few minutes passed before he opened the door. Evidently, he had just gotten out of the shower and was naked when she knocked. Now he was barefoot, and the unbuttoned waistband of his jeans revealed his flat, muscular stomach and a shadowy line of silky dark hair. His naked shoulders were gilded by the lamplight, and water gleamed on his tousled chestnut hair. He looked powerful, virile—and half angry.

"How come you're still here?" he demanded.

"The others had gone before I received your message. Is Amanda's Baby all right?"

"Just bruised. Another horse bolted and hit her in the shoulder. Thank God it didn't happen before the race. But we had a vet give her a thorough going over, of course."

"I'm glad she's not hurt. I—I wanted to explain something about this afternoon. . . ."

People were coming and going along the balcony walkway that led to the second-story rooms. Barr's glance raked over her, and then he opened the door wider.

"Come inside."

"No, I can tell you from here. . . ."

"Come inside." He caught her by the elbow. The grip wasn't harsh enough to be painful, but there was a warning in it. He was in no mood for resistance or argument.

Vickie stepped stiffly inside. "I wanted to explain why I didn't bet on Amanda's Baby. It wasn't because I didn't want her to win. I just got this sudden superstitious flash that if I bet on her, she *wouldn't* win. I know it was foolish. It's attaching too much importance to oneself to think what you do or don't do could actually influence some outside event."

Barr snatched up the towel he had flung in a chair when he answered the door. She watched the hard ripple of muscles under his tanned skin, magnificent as any race horse's, while he toweled his hair dry.

"Who knows what controls the tides of fate?" he muttered finally. "Have you eaten?"

"No, I haven't." Vickie's held breath escaped in relief. Eating was an easy excuse to leave the intimacy of his room. She was all too aware of the proximity of the queen-sized bed, the half nakedness of Barr's hard, masculine body—and the fact that everyone else had already gone back to the ranch. And she was electrically aware that behind Barr's inscrutable mask he was not indifferent to those facts, either. Her breathing felt strange, as if a band were wrapped around her chest. Yes, she needed the safety of numbers in the big dining room!

She didn't realize what Barr intended until he was already on the phone placing an order to have room service deliver a meal to the room. He cocked an eyebrow at Vickie's shocked expression when he put down the phone.

"My choice of broiled lobster was not satisfactory?"

"I thought we'd go to the dining room!"

"I have to call the ranch, of course, and I'm expecting another phone call." As if on cue, the phone rang. "Make yourself comfortable." He waved a negligent hand at an easy chair.

Vickie perched uneasily on the edge of the chair and flipped unseeingly through a promotional pamphlet about the area and the races. He called the ranch after the first call ended, and then the phone rang again. He was still talking when room service delivered the meal. He signed for it and handed the boy a generous tip.

The phone rang yet again as they were eating, someone offering congratulations, and Barr countered with an invitation to the celebration at the ranch. Vickie relaxed as she ate the succulent, butter-drenched lobster. With the phone so busy, Barr wouldn't have time for the tantalizing possibilities that lurked like a secret treasure—or trap!—in Vickie's mind.

"That was truly a marvelous dinner," Vickie said brightly when she was finished. She stood up. The phone rang again, a convenient time to make a graceful exit. "So I'll see you in the morning. . . ."

He yanked the cord to the phone out of its jack, and the sound died in midring. She stared at him with wide eyes and parted lips as she took a panicky step backward toward the door, then another.

He trapped her at the door, a powerful arm braced on either side of her as she pressed her hands and back against the wooden barrier.

"I think your idea of moving the celebration back to the ranch so your mother can enjoy it was very thoughtful," she said inanely. "And thank you for the lovely meal."

His hands moved in to imprison her slender throat. "I'm still hungry." Seeing her astonished expression, he laughed softly. "I'm hungry for you, Victoria Wildcat Thornton. And don't tell me that all you've had on your mind this evening is how delicious the lobster tasted. I saw you eyeing the bed. In fact, I really think you should have a closer view!"

She gave a small cry as he scooped her up in his arms and carried her to the bed. His naked shoulder felt warm against her cheek. He deposited her on the bed and trapped her there with his body, as if he expected her to fight to escape. He ran his fingers through the shining curtain of her hair and then framed her face with his hands.

"Here we are again," he said huskily.

Yes, she echoed tremulously. *Here we are again.* His lean male body fit into her feminine curves and hollows as if it belonged there. There was a warm familiarity to the fit, yet she was thrillingly aware of the unknown lurking behind the familiarity. A dangerous unknown, one she had warned herself repeatedly she must not explore, yet her body felt pliable, boneless, softening to meet his advance with no more resistance than a shimmering surface of silvery water. Her arms wound around his neck, and he kissed her closed eyelids.

"I can't help wondering, if you're so much in love with him, how come you keep winding up in my arms," he growled. He sounded angry and resentful, but his touch was sweet fire. "You drive me wild! You act as if you want to love me as much as I want to love you, and then suddenly you run or tell me no."

Vickie's palms slid over the powerful muscles of his back and found the hard ridge of his spine. "There are others who wouldn't tell you no." Her eyes looked into the depths of his, dark as a green sea lashed by storm.

"I don't want others!" he said fiercely. "I want *you*. You know damn well the only reason I accepted Lou Ann's invitation was because I was so frustrated with you and that call from the ex-husband you're still in love with."

"Where is Lou Ann this weekend?"

"I don't know. Around somewhere, I guess."

He sounded annoyed, frustrated by her introduction of a subject that didn't interest him. His mouth abruptly enveloped hers as if to silence or punish her. The kiss did indeed silence her, but it was no punishment. It sent her senses soaring, climbing to a place where she was conscious only of the river of oneness flowing between them. It had a depth, a power that swept her along. But she was not helpless in the current. She went with it willingly.

"Stay with me tonight," he whispered against her lips.

"Are you going to promise me again that nothing will happen?"

He raised up to look down at her. "No," he said softly.

"You're determined to make love to me because you won't admit defeat. If you see a challenge, you have to meet and conquer it! And I'm a challenge you haven't yet conquered."

He flung himself away from her angrily, then trapped her with an arm and leg thrown over her before she could escape. "This sounds like a rerun of Phoenix," he muttered.

"Nothing has changed since Phoenix!"

"That's right. I wanted you in Phoenix, and I want you now. You wanted me in Phoenix, and you want me now." His voice was ragged. "And I'm not going to let your crazy, mixed-up ideas come between us again!"

His leg moved up to imprison her against the bed, and his hands fumbled impatiently with the buttons of her blouse. Roughly, he swept the blouse and sheer bra away, but some of his frustrated rage softened when he saw her pink-tipped breasts vulnerably exposed to his gaze and hands. He cupped and squeezed her right breast gently, then moved to caress the other one with equal tenderness. He circled the rosy peak with his tongue.

"Vickie, I want to make love to you," he whispered huskily. "It seems as if I've waited all my life to make love to you." His voice turned urgent. "I know you have some wild idea that I want you only because you're some kind of challenge to my male ego. . . ."

He broke off and lifted his head to look down at her. Her eyes felt heavy-lidded, but not with sleep. Desire made them languid and soft. His finger tips brushed her lips, and she kissed them.

"And maybe there is a little truth in what you say. You are a challenge to me!" he admitted. "But not the way you think. You're more important to me than I ever thought any woman could be. I'm falling in love with you—and I can't make you love me! It's a challenge I don't know how to conquer."

But you have conquered it, and me, Vickie thought. She ran her finger tips over the chestnut arch of his eyebrows and the small lines of frustration between them.

"I don't know how to compete with this—this other man," he went on. "I feel as if I'm shadowboxing. Fighting with ghosts I can't see!"

Vickie's mind lingered on the words that had come before, words that were both a ray of joy and a stab of pain. A bitter-sweet pleasure. He was falling in love with her. An opening in heaven—and then a cruel closing. Because it was too late. The wheels were in motion for tomorrow night. It had always been too late for them.

But there was tonight. One night to remember forever. . . .

"You don't have to compete," she said softly. "There is no other man. No ghost."

"I don't understand what you're saying." He sounded wary, suspicious. As if he thought this was some new trick to turn him away again.

"There is no ex-husband," she said simply. "There is no other man I love. There is no man in the world I've ever loved even a fraction as much as I love you."

"Vickie, if this is some kind of trick—" he began warningly. He moved his hand back to her breast as if it were a reflex action. She felt the warmth and closeness of the small, absent-minded circling of finger tips around the exquisitely sensitive nipple.

"I tried to tell you in Phoenix. But you jumped to the wrong conclusion, and then everything went wrong."

"Why did you lie to me about being married before?" He sounded as if he still doubted her.

"To help me get the job on the ranch," she answered honestly.

He considered that, while at the same time his hand continued to wander over her as if some secret instruc-

169

tion willed it to leave no inch untouched. "But there's more," he said finally. "If that was all there was, you could have told me before this. There was the man on the phone. . . ."

"Yes. There's more." She had always known he would unerringly leap to that fact.

"Will you tell me what it is?"

She couldn't tell him. But she could no longer lie to him either. "No," she said simply.

He looked more bewildered than angry. He obviously had not even the most remote suspicion of the truth about her. "Will you tell me everything someday?"

Vickie felt a shudder of raw pain. "You'll understand everything very soon," she said in a whisper so low that it was more a transmission of thought than spoken words.

He turned her face to his and kissed her softly on the mouth. She realized brokenly that he thought her whisper was an agreement to his request. He didn't realize it was a simple truth. Soon he would understand everything. And hate her for what she had done.

"You're a mysterious little wildcat, do you know that?"

"Do you still want to make love to a—a mysterious wildcat?" she asked tremulously. Just for tonight she would pretend that this was a beginning, not an end.

His answer was fervent. "More than anything in the world."

His hand slid to the waistband of her slacks. The zipper made a soft rustle as he slid it down. His hand, eager but unhurried, found the flat plane of her abdomen and delighted in the satin skin and rounded curve of hipbone. He lifted her body with one strong arm and started to work the slacks over her hips. She stopped him with a light hand on his wrist.

"I—I told you I've never been married." She felt a

170

small flush of self-consciousness, almost as if she were admitting something shameful. "I've never even . . ."

She let the words trail off, but he understood instantly. His eyes widened in surprise. He smoothed the material over the curve of her hip.

"You don't want me now because of what I've told you?" she asked in dismay.

"Oh, Vickie, sweetheart, I want you. More than you can know." He rolled to one side and let his hand roam her half-naked body in long strokes, as if storing up the memory. "But I want you for much, much longer than tonight. And I can be patient a little longer for a real wedding night."

He kissed her again, a kiss so filled with sweet promise that it brought a shimmer of tears to her eyes.

The one thing she wanted more than anything in the world was within her reach—but after tomorrow night, forever out of her grasp.

And she was to be denied even this one night of love to cherish in her memory.

Chapter Ten

The flight back to the ranch the following morning was
uneventful except that Barr's gaze and frequent touch
were warm and loving. Vickie had spent the night alone
in her room, he in his. Smiling ruefully, he had said that
would be best because his will power wasn't operating
at top efficiency and he doubted it was up to the
temptation of having her in his arms all night.

He was still curious, that was obvious, but he was
willing to wait for her explanation. There was even a
kind of protectiveness about his patience. How soon
that would all change, Vickie thought with a leaden
weight of despair.

The ranch was already a humming beehive of activity
when they arrived. An immense barbecue grill had
been set up on the patio. People were already arriving
and were quickly drafted to help with preparations.
Music blared from a loudspeaker connected to the
stereo system.

By midafternoon, delicious smells drifted up from
the barbecue. The swimming pool overflowed with
laughing, shouting people. Amanda accepted congratulations in a chair set up in the shade for her. A
three-piece western band arrived and started playing.
More and more people arrived, eager to help the

Chandlers celebrate, and there was laughter and noise and gaiety. Someone released a gay cloud of balloons.

Vickie saw it all, smiled, helped wherever she could, but she felt apart from the jubilation. There was an invisible but impregnable wall between her and all the gaiety and laughter. She slipped away to her room and packed her belongings, taking only a few items at a time to her car so as not to arouse suspicion. But caution wasn't all that necessary. There was so much camaraderie, so many activities going on, that Vickie suspected, with grim humor, that she could have hauled out the living-room furniture and people would simply have offered to give her a hand.

Amanda's Baby arrived in a luxurious van. She showed no sign of her slight injury as she stepped down the ramp from the padded van. She looked every inch the proud racing queen she was, with arched neck and flaring nostrils, but when the trainer led her up to Mrs. Chandler, the big filly dropped her velvet nose to the woman's lap. Mrs. Chandler hugged her like a girl and cried with happiness. Then the filly was given her own place of honor in a nearby corral. She delighted everyone by being so curious about her own welcoming banner that she soon had it underfoot on the ground.

Vickie helped serve the food. People were still eating when darkness drifted in and the band readied for real dancing. Fireworks, brought in by some overexuberant guest, sporadically lit the sky with explosions of color.

Finally, Vickie slipped away in the darkness to locate the pickup Kathy had said they would be driving. Vickie had told Kathy to park around by the big barn, but there were dozens of other vehicles parked there, also, Mercedes and old trucks, luxury motor homes and beat-up campers. Many of the celebrants evidently planned to spend the night.

Then Kathy's soft voice called to Vickie, guiding her

to the nondescript pickup that blended in perfectly with the other vehicles. Al, the expert at this, lounged by the fender. In his scuffed boots and broad-brimmed hat, he looked as if he belonged there. Kathy's face was pinched and nervous, but her eyes glowed. In low voices, they laid the final plans under Al's direction.

An hour later, the plans were carried out. Everything went smoothly. Vickie offered to put the children to bed. They were surprised and curious, but not alarmed, when Vickie took them to the waiting pickup instead of to bed. Vickie hadn't time to judge their reaction to Kathy's hugs and tears. In moments, the pickup was gone, just one more in the irregular stream of vehicles coming and going. Vickie was a bit dismayed to learn that Kathy planned to take the children to Amarillo only long enough for Aunt Verla to see them, then spirit them off somewhere Ric couldn't find them. But it was out of her hands now.

Vickie hurried inside and gathered up the last of her things. She fought a temptation to go to Barr for the sweet pain of one last word or kiss. She knew she must not do it. She might break down and give away everything. At the last minute, she left a brief unsigned note in Benji's room saying that Kathy had the children now. She was afraid that Kathy would forget her promise to call the Chandlers, and Vickie still couldn't bear the thought of their thinking the children had been harmed.

Then Vickie slid into her car and drove away. Behind her, the sounds of music and laughter drifted out to fill the immense, lonely land with celebration. She felt as if some switch within her had been set on automatic, and if it was turned off, she would stumble to a halt, like some wound-down robot. Her last thought as she drove under the Chandler sign at the edge of the ranch was that this truly was the Valley of Broken Hearts. Hers felt as if it were shattered into a million jagged pieces, and each one cut like a sliver of steel into the core of her being.

The moon had not yet risen, but a glow on the horizon heralded its coming. Vickie drove steadily, neither fast nor slow. She passed a few cars, but the road was lightly traveled. Everyone, she thought wryly, was already at the Chandlers'. And when, she wondered bleakly, would Barr realize that she was gone?

She slowed down when she saw a vehicle angled into the ditch up ahead. One wheel was crumpled against a utility pole. She was past the pickup before she realized that even in its nondescript dustiness it looked a little familiar. Frighteningly familiar. No, it couldn't be. . . .

She drove another half mile before she knew she had to turn around and check. As she drove up, a familiar little face was pressed against the window, then quickly jerked away. She parked her car on the edge of the road, and leaving the lights on, ran up to the pickup. The door opened, and Kathy and the kids spilled out. Susan gave a strangled little cry and grabbed Vickie around the legs. In the glare of the headlights, Benji's face was tear-stained. Kathy was trembling.

"Kitten! Oh, my Lord, I'm so glad it's you! I was so afraid it was Ric coming after us. . . ."

"Kathy, what happened?" Vickie asked.

Some crazy cowboy had come barreling down the road and forced them into the ditch. The axle was bent when the pickup hit the utility pole, and the pickup wouldn't move. The contrite cowboy had taken Al to the next small town where Kathy's car was parked. Kathy and Al had brought two vehicles, planning to switch the children to the second one as a safety precaution in case the pickup was spotted or remembered by someone.

Headlights approached from the direction of the

ranch. They slowed, and Kathy's reaction was one of pure terror. She was close to hysteria, Vickie realized. The children were crying and clinging to Vickie. Somehow Vickie managed to call a calm assurance to a shouted question from someone in the car that everything was fine. The car moved on. Kathy leaned weakly against the pickup, her shoulders shuddering convulsively.

"Kitten, what have they done to my children?" She sobbed brokenly. "Benji keeps asking if we're all in heaven now. I don't think Susan even knows who I am!"

Kathy could be right, Vickie thought helplessly as Susan clung to her leg. At this moment, Vickie was a more familiar figure to the children than was this other strange, crying woman who claimed to be their mother. Damn Ric and his lie!

"Ric is going to come after them," Kathy said. "I know he is! He'll take the kids, and I'll never see them again!"

That was possible, Vickie thought, catching some of Kathy's panic. But in the back of her mind was the odd, disloyal thought that this was exactly what Kathy planned to do: take the children where *Ric* couldn't see them again.

"I want grandma!" Susan shrilled when Kathy tried to pick her up.

What a horrible, horrible mess, Vickie thought. She felt bewildered and helpless, trapped and somehow responsible for all this. If the note she'd left in Benji's room was found tonight, the Chandlers would surely come searching for the kids.

"Kitten, you take the kids," Kathy said urgently. "I'll have to get reacquainted with them later. They're just scared of me now. Take them to mom's and I'll come there when Al gets back here with my car. But we've got to get them out of here before Ric comes along."

Reluctantly, Vickie nodded. At the moment, it seemed the thing to do. The kids were scared and bewildered, and Vickie wasn't sure she was thinking any too clearly herself. The situation seemed theatrical and unreal there in the blazing glare of the headlights.

The children went with Vickie willingly. Kathy climbed back in the pickup to wait for Al. In the car, the kids were asleep in minutes, Susan snuggled up against Vickie, Benji leaning against his little sister.

Poor kids, Vickie thought, blinking back tears of her own as she looked down at their tear-stained little faces. Poor Kathy, shocked and upset by her children's uncertain reaction to her after the long separation. Poor Ric, too, who would soon learn the children were gone.

At the intersection with the main east-west highway across New Mexico, Vickie hesitated, torn. Her thoughts were ragged and unformed, but she had the growing and inescapable conviction that this was all wrong. *Wrong.* Did the children simply belong back at the ranch, permanently separated from their mother? No! Ric had been unfair and wrong in taking them. But this was wrong, too!

So what was *right*?

Vickie was suddenly too exhausted and bewildered to know. She turned left, and minutes later the lights of Albuquerque were spread out below the slope of highway. She found an anonymous-looking motel, not thinking until too late that perhaps she shouldn't have registered under her real name. She bathed the children's faces, answered their bewildered questions, wiped away their tears and tucked them in bed in their underthings, since she had nothing else for them to wear.

177

There was instant coffee and a tiny hot plate for heating water. Vickie made a strong cup and curled up in the room's only chair. She was indescribably weary, but thoughts bolted back and forth through her mind without letup.

She saw a terrible pattern of destruction developing. First Ric had snatched the children. Now Kathy had taken them. Vickie knew it wouldn't end there. Vickie doubted that Kathy could hide from the Chandler money and determination indefinitely. Or if she did manage to keep the children hidden, it would be at the expense of their childhood freedom, always fearful Ric might take them—legally or illegally. If he did get them, he'd make sure Kathy never got near them again. And there was the ugly possibility one or both parents would eventually wind up with criminal charges or penalties in this private war. The kids came out losers no matter which parent "won."

It was, in Barr's own words, a no-win situation. An ugly, desperate, impossible situation. She realized that neither Kathy or Ric were bad people in spite of the things they had done. They loved their children, but they were human and very fallible. Sometimes right, sometimes wrong. And somehow the destructive pattern had to be stopped before it caused irreparable damage to the kids.

That was the one thought that emerged strong and clear from the confusion of Vickie's jumbled thoughts as she sat there with her coffee and the sounds of the children's soft, vulnerable breathing. Susan's and Benji's well-being and interests must come first, ahead of anything either Kathy or Ric wanted.

And how to accomplish that? What *was* best for Benji and Susan? Vickie felt more helpless than ever. She had a decision as difficult as the one King Solomon had once made about a child, but she did not have King Solomon's wisdom or experience.

She fell asleep in the chair and woke cramped and stiff with the weak light of first dawn creeping into the room.

The problem was still there. Nothing had changed. Kathy was probably in Amarillo by now, frantic because Vickie and the children hadn't arrived there. Ric was undoubtedly frantic, too, knowing by now that the children were gone. And Barr? Barr was no doubt seething with an icy fury.

Vickie must decide what to do. And she didn't know what to do, didn't know what was right or best. At the moment, she didn't even know what was *least* wrong, least undesirable.

Barr would know what to do. The thought hit her like a blinding light, and she bathed in the momentary luxury of relief. Then the light dimmed. Barr had that fierce, ruthless loyalty to his own family. He wouldn't be fair to Kathy!

But the children were his family, also, some other part of her mind argued. Wouldn't he feel just as much loyalty toward them, just as much responsibility and concern to see that what was best for *them* was done? Or would he? Would his bitterness at Vickie's role in the deception cloud his basic sense of justice and prejudice him against what was best for the children?

In the end, she could only trust and hope that he cared as much about the children's welfare as she did and that he would put that above the fury and bitterness he undoubtedly felt toward Vickie herself.

The inexpensive motel room had no phone. Vickie checked the children to be sure they were still sleeping soundly, then found a phone booth outside. The morning was clear and cool, almost chill. She hadn't enough change to make the call and placed it collect, person-to-person to Barr. He was on the line almost before she was prepared for him.

"This—this is Vickie," she said.

"So the operator just informed me." His voice was taut, a little mocking. She closed her eyes, seeing his rugged figure and harshly unwavering expression. *She* was far outside his protective concern now.

"You know by now that the children are gone?"

"Ric found a note when he went to look in on them before breakfast this morning. *Your* note, I presume?"

"Yes. I—I didn't want any of you to worry that something terrible had happened to them."

"How thoughtful of you." His voice dripped acid.

"I—" She swallowed convulsively. "I need your help."

"First," he said grimly, "the time for explanations has come. No more evasions. No more half truths. The *truth. All* of it."

Haltingly, Vickie struggled through that truth, her relationship with Kathy and Aunt Verla, why she had come to the ranch, trying to make him understand the background of why she'd done what she had, why she *had* to help Kathy get her children back. He said nothing beyond an occasional remote, "I see."

When she finished, there was a long silence before he asked, "So why did you call *me?*"

"Because I didn't know who else to turn to," she cried. Because I love you, her heart echoed. Then she rushed on, half afraid he would hang up before she could tell him her doubts and fears for the children and her conviction that this destructive pattern must be broken.

"Everything you say may very well be true. I've had some of the same thoughts myself." Barr's response was cold even though his words held agreement. "But

180

I'm afraid that's immaterial now. Kathy has the children."

Vickie took a deep breath and closed her eyes, feeling as if she were stepping off into empty space. "No, she doesn't. I have Susan and Benji."

"What?"

More explanations and finally a wary repetition of what he had asked earlier. Why had she called him?

"Because I don't know what to do!" she cried. "Because I thought—hoped—you could be fair."

"No other reason?"

"What other reason could there be?"

There was a small hesitation before he said almost bitterly, "Not long ago you said you loved me."

"Yes." Her voice was weary and broken. "And I love Kathy and Aunt Verla and the kids, too. No matter what I did, I betrayed someone I loved."

Silence.

"But there must be something better than this awful mess," she went on desperately. "Perhaps Ric and Kathy could be made to see the damage they're doing the children. Perhaps they could work out a reasonable legal-custody agreement that would enable both of them to share their children's lives. I don't know! *Help me!*"

Another long silence. Then he asked for the name and address of the motel where she was staying. She hesitated for a long moment. Once she told him, she and the children were in his power. Finally, taking a shaky breath, she told him.

There, it was done. "Wh-what are you going to do?" she asked tremulously.

"I don't know yet." He hesitated. "You're—all right?" The question was wary, with none of the loving tenderness of that last night in Ruidoso.

"Just fine." She couldn't keep the irony out of her

voice. Her heart was breaking, her world in shambles. But she was "fine."

She hung up the receiver and braced her head against the phone to gather strength to walk back to the motel room.

After that, she could only wait. She took the children out for breakfast and bought some clean clothes for them at a nearby market. They watched television and took a short walk after lunch. Later, she bought sleepers for them, as it appeared they would be spending another night in the bleak motel.

What was going to happen? She had no idea what to expect. She had a vague inkling that what she had done with the children might very well be labeled kidnaping. Would the police, alerted by Barr, barge in and place her under arrest?

She felt as alone as if she were on an alien planet. Alone and hated, because by now Kathy must hate her for the betrayal. She had already felt Barr's bitterness over the phone. She had failed and betrayed everyone she loved. Perhaps Barr and Ric would come and simply take the children by force. She couldn't stop them. How could she ever face Kathy then? Had she let her love for Barr blur her view of him? Had she given him qualities of compassion and caring and justice that he did not possess?

The night was black. So black and long.

Another morning. Another breakfast. The children were tiring of this strange game, but, surprisingly, Benji talked often about his mother. Seeing her had awakened memories. He talked of things he and his mother and even Aunt Verla had done. Susan asked curious little questions. Vickie explained that Kathy had never been in heaven, that that was just a mistake. Benji asked if they would see their mother again soon. Vickie couldn't answer.

That evening, the three of them were watching television together when a knock sounded on the door. Vickie's heart gave a leap of panic. She steadied herself and went to the door.

"Who is it?" she asked through the still-closed door.

"Barr."

She opened the door. Before she could say anything, the kids gave glad cries of recognition and raced to him. He knelt down and put an arm around each of them.

"Have you two been good kids? You haven't been giving Vickie any problems?"

"I saw my mommy," Benji announced importantly. "She didn't go away to heaven."

"I know. And you know something else? She's waiting out in the car for you. And your dad is there, too." Vickie saw his arms tighten to prevent the children from immediately dashing to the car. "Is that all right with you?" His voice changed as he spoke to Vickie, the gentle warmth turning to a glitter of cold steel.

"They're in the *same* car?"

"Yes."

She nodded, and he released the children. They shot toward the waiting car.

"How did you manage *that?*" Vickie asked in astonishment as she saw both doors of the waiting car open to receive the children.

"I called Kathy as soon as I heard from you, and then Rick and I flew over to Amarillo. I told both of them that Susan and Benji were safe, but I was not going to tell them where the kids were until they sat down and talked sensibly and made some reasonable decisions about what was best for their children. I figured if you could take drastic measures, so could I. They've been talking practically nonstop ever since."

"They worked out a custody agreement?"

183

The dim, yellowish light outside the motel door gleamed on the sunlit streaks of his chestnut hair, turning them golden. "They worked out a *marriage* agreement. They're going back together." He allowed himself a small smile of satisfaction as he turned to look back at the car. It was a smile that somehow excluded Vickie, and it was gone when he turned back to her.

"Do you think it will work?" Vickie asked hopefully. She made a resolute effort to think only of the reunited family and not of the man standing at her door, so close and yet so far away.

"They've grown up a lot. They know they've both made mistakes, but I don't think they ever stopped loving each other. I think they'll make it work."

Vickie nodded. In all Kathy's anger and despair, Vickie had never once actually heard Kathy say that she no longer loved Ric. "I'm happy for them. And I want to thank you for your—your cooperation." She swallowed a constricting pain in her throat. "I guess that takes care of everything then. . . ."

"No, it doesn't. Not by a long shot it doesn't," he said grimly. With an open palm, he shoved her backward and swiftly stepped inside and closed the door.

"You have no right. . . ."

"I'll make my own rights!"

She retreated behind the chair in which she had spent that first long, restless night. "What do you want?"

He simply looked at her with narrowed eyes and made no answer.

"Ric and Kathy are waiting in the car for you!" she cried, panicked by the hard inscrutability of his expression.

"No." The word was flat. "I told them that as soon as I came inside and closed the door, they could leave." He took a step toward the barrier of the chair between them. "You deceived me. Every day, every hour, every minute, you deceived me! Even in my arms, you deceived me."

"I had no choice!"

"That night in Ruidoso when you told me the truth—a part of the truth—and then refused to tell me more . . ." He smiled grimly. "I imagined a dozen wild things about you. A criminal past. Blackmail. And I decided whatever it was, it didn't matter, because I loved you."

Loved you. Past tense. "But this matters," she said dully.

"I never felt more betrayed in my life than when I saw your note and got your call and realized that everything about you was phony. Everything you'd ever done or said to me was all part of the big act."

"No!"

"Your teasing little yes-and-no game was especially effective. You had me so crazy mixed up I didn't know whether I was coming or going. The perfect way to divert my attention from your real purpose on the ranch! And I fell for it. All the way. I never once suspected the truth about you. Congratulations," he added contemptuously.

Vickie just shook her head helplessly. Yet she couldn't simply bow her head and accept everything he heaped on her! "It wasn't all an act," she said fiercely.

"Wasn't it? First you're the experienced divorcée fed up with men and love. When that got old, you were the *brokenhearted* divorcée still in love with your ex-husband. . . ."

"I never said that. You jumped to that conclusion yourself."

He paid no attention. "And then you were the innocent little virgin, willing but shy." He smiled mirthlessly, his voice mocking and a dark glitter in his eyes. "Well, Little Miss Wildcat, I think I'll now find out *exactly* what you are."

With one slashing gesture, he flung the chair aside. It crashed to the floor. Vickie cringed backward. There was a fire of menacing determination in his eyes.

Then, slowly, she straightened and squared her shoulders.

"Yes," she agreed with raw defiance, her eyes meeting his. Recklessly, her hands went to the buttons of her blouse. The blouse slipped unheeded to the floor, and the lacy scrap of her bra followed. The lamplight gleamed on the pearly translucence of her skin. He stood transfixed, as if he wanted to stop her but couldn't. "Find out what I am! Find out that at the last I told you the truth. And I told the truth whenever I could without betraying the people who loved and depended on me!"

A flicker of doubt crossed his harsh expression.

"I'm sorry I had to deceive you. But I had no choice. When I agreed to help Kathy and Aunt Verla, I had no idea that I would—" She broke off abruptly.

"Would what?" he prodded relentlessly.

"Fall in love with you." Her mouth trembled, but the proud defiance of her stance did not falter. "And then when I did fall in love with you, I was trapped, knowing that no matter what I did, I betrayed someone I loved."

He shook his head, an uncharacteristic uncertainty in his expression. "I'm not sure what to believe. . . ."

"Stay with me tonight." Vickie walked to the bed and flung the covers back. "In the past, you've asked me to stay with you. Now I'm making the invitation!"

"No!"

Vickie reeled as if she had been shot. He stepped forward and caught her by the arms to hold her upright.

Her head sagged against his shoulder, but he forced it to tilt up to meet his gaze.

"Vickie, do you remember I once told you I hadn't married because I'd never met the woman I couldn't live without and I wouldn't marry for any less important a reason?" His hands tightened on her arms. "I've met her now. I accused you of betrayal, but you never betrayed your basic convictions of loyalty and responsibility and concern—and love. You were willing to risk everything when you knew the children were being wronged." He took a deep breath. "I don't want to spend just one night with you, Miss Vickie Wildcat Thornton with the iron principles." His voice was fierce. "I want to spend a lifetime with you. I want to start out fresh, with no deceptions."

"No deceptions," Vickie agreed fervently. "No deceptions ever again." The numbness was going out of her. She felt a singing in her heart, and the heat of Barr's male body suddenly pressed against her naked breasts. And then she made the most honest statement she had ever made in her life. "I love you."

"Enough to wait just a little longer—until we can be married?" he challenged.

"Enough to wait as long as you want me to," she said simply.

"I love you." His slow smile held a lifetime of sweet promise. "I love you."

Silhouette Romance

IT'S YOUR OWN SPECIAL TIME
Contemporary romances for today's women.
Each month, six very special love stories will be yours
from SILHOUETTE. Look for them wherever books are sold
or order now from the coupon below.

$1.50 each

☐ 5 Goforth	☐ 28 Hampson	☐ 54 Beckman	☐ 83 Halston
☐ 6 Stanford	☐ 29 Wildman	☐ 55 LaDame	☐ 84 Vitek
☐ 7 Lewis	☐ 30 Dixon	☐ 56 Trent	☐ 85 John
☐ 8 Beckman	☐ 32 Michaels	☐ 57 John	☐ 86 Adams
☐ 9 Wilson	☐ 33 Vitek	☐ 58 Stanford	☐ 87 Michaels
☐ 10 Caine	☐ 34 John	☐ 59 Vernon	☐ 88 Stanford
☐ 11 Vernon	☐ 35 Stanford	☐ 60 Hill	☐ 89 James
☐ 17 John	☐ 38 Browning	☐ 61 Michaels	☐ 90 Major
☐ 19 Thornton	☐ 39 Sinclair	☐ 62 Halston	☐ 92 McKay
☐ 20 Fulford	☐ 46 Stanford	☐ 63 Brent	☐ 93 Browning
☐ 22 Stephens	☐ 47 Vitek	☐ 71 Ripy	☐ 94 Hampson
☐ 23 Edwards	☐ 48 Wildman	☐ 73 Browning	☐ 95 Wisdom
☐ 24 Healy	☐ 49 Wisdom	☐ 76 Hardy	☐ 96 Beckman
☐ 25 Stanford	☐ 50 Scott	☐ 78 Oliver	☐ 97 Clay
☐ 26 Hastings	☐ 52 Hampson	☐ 81 Roberts	☐ 98 St. George
☐ 27 Hampson	☐ 53 Browning	☐ 82 Dailey	☐ 99 Camp

$1.75 each

☐ 100 Stanford	☐ 114 Michaels	☐ 128 Hampson	☐ 143 Roberts
☐ 101 Hardy	☐ 115 John	☐ 129 Converse	☐ 144 Goforth
☐ 102 Hastings	☐ 116 Lindley	☐ 130 Hardy	☐ 145 Hope
☐ 103 Cork	☐ 117 Scott	☐ 131 Stanford	☐ 146 Michaels
☐ 104 Vitek	☐ 118 Dailey	☐ 132 Wisdom	☐ 147 Hampson
☐ 105 Eden	☐ 119 Hampson	☐ 133 Rowe	☐ 148 Cork
☐ 106 Dailey	☐ 120 Carroll	☐ 134 Charles	☐ 149 Saunders
☐ 107 Bright	☐ 121 Langan	☐ 135 Logan	☐ 150 Major
☐ 108 Hampson	☐ 122 Scofield	☐ 136 Hampson	☐ 151 Hampson
☐ 109 Vernon	☐ 123 Sinclair	☐ 137 Hunter	☐ 152 Halston
☐ 110 Trent	☐ 124 Beckman	☐ 138 Wilson	☐ 153 Dailey
☐ 111 South	☐ 125 Bright	☐ 139 Vitek	☐ 154 Beckman
☐ 112 Stanford	☐ 126 St. George	☐ 140 Erskine	☐ 155 Hampson
☐ 113 Browning	☐ 127 Roberts	☐ 142 Browning	☐ 156 Sawyer

$1.75 each

- ☐ 157 Vitek
- ☐ 158 Reynolds
- ☐ 159 Tracy
- ☐ 160 Hampson
- ☐ 161 Trent
- ☐ 162 Ashby
- ☐ 163 Roberts
- ☐ 164 Browning
- ☐ 165 Young
- ☐ 166 Wisdom
- ☐ 167 Hunter
- ☐ 168 Carr
- ☐ 169 Scott

- ☐ 170 Ripy
- ☐ 171 Hill
- ☐ 172 Browning
- ☐ 173 Camp
- ☐ 174 Sinclair
- ☐ 175 Jarrett
- ☐ 176 Vitek
- ☐ 177 Dailey
- ☐ 178 Hampson
- ☐ 179 Beckman
- ☐ 180 Roberts
- ☐ 181 Terrill
- ☐ 182 Clay

- ☐ 183 Stanley
- ☐ 184 Hardy
- ☐ 185 Hampson
- ☐ 186 Howard
- ☐ 187 Scott
- ☐ 188 Cork
- ☐ 189 Stephens
- ☐ 190 Hampson
- ☐ 191 Browning
- ☐ 192 John
- ☐ 193 Trent
- ☐ 194 Barry
- ☐ 195 Dailey

- ☐ 196 Hampson
- ☐ 197 Summers
- ☐ 198 Hunter
- ☐ 199 Roberts
- ☐ 200 Lloyd
- ☐ 201 Starr
- ☐ 202 Hampson
- ☐ 203 Browning
- ☐ 204 Carroll
- ☐ 205 Maxam
- ☐ 206 Manning
- ☐ 207 Windham

$1.95 each

- ☐ 208 Halston
- ☐ 209 LaDame
- ☐ 210 Eden
- ☐ 211 Walters
- ☐ 212 Young
- ☐ 213 Dailey

- ☐ 214 Hampson
- ☐ 215 Roberts
- ☐ 216 Saunders
- ☐ 217 Vitek
- ☐ 218 Hunter
- ☐ 219 Cork

- ☐ 220 Hampson
- ☐ 221 Browning
- ☐ 222 Carroll
- ☐ 223 Summers
- ☐ 224 Langan
- ☐ 225 St. George

- ☐ 226 Hampson
- ☐ 227 Beckman
- ☐ 228 King
- ☐ 229 Thornton
- ☐ 230 Stevens
- ☐ 231 Dailey

- _#232 SPELL OF THE ISLAND, Hampson
- _#233 EDGE OF PARADISE, Vernon
- _#234 NEXT YEAR'S BLONDE, Smith
- _#235 NO EASY CONQUEST, James
- _#236 LOST IN LOVE, Maxam
- _#237 WINTER PROMISE, Wilson

- _#238 OUTBACK DREAMING, Cork
- _#239 VALLEY OF BROKEN HEARTS, McKay
- _#240 SHARED DESTINY, Hunter
- _#241 SNOW QUEEN, Wisdom
- _#242 NO GUARANTEES, Brooke
- _#243 THE LANGUAGE OF LOVE, Saunders

SILHOUETTE BOOKS, Department SB/1
1230 Avenue of the Americas
New York, NY 10020

Please send me the books I have checked above. I am enclosing $_____
(please add 50¢ to cover postage and handling. NYS and NYC residents please
add appropriate sales tax). Send check or money order—no cash or C.O.D.'s
please. Allow six weeks for delivery.

NAME _____

ADDRESS _____

CITY _____ STATE/ZIP _____

Love, passion and adventure will be yours FREE for 15 days... with Tapestry™ historical romances!

"Long before women could read and write, tapestries were used to record events and stories . . . especially the exploits of courageous knights and their ladies."

And now there's a new kind of tapestry...

In the pages of Tapestry™ romance novels, you'll find love, intrigue, and historical touches that really make the stories come alive!

You'll meet brave Guyon d'Arcy, a Norman knight . . . handsome Comte Andre de Crillon, a Huguenot royalist . . . rugged Branch Taggart, a feuding American rancher . . . and more. And on each journey back in time, you'll experience tender romance and searing passion . . . and learn about the way people lived and loved in earlier times than ours.

We think you'll be so delighted with Tapestry romances, you won't want to miss a single one! We'd like to send you 2 books each month, as soon as they are published, through our Tapestry Home Subscription Service.℠ Look them over for 15 days, free. If not delighted, simply return them and owe nothing. But if you enjoy them as much as we think you will, pay the invoice enclosed. There's never any additional charge for this convenient service — we pay all postage and handling costs.

To receive your Tapestry historical romances, fill out the coupon below and mail it to us today. You're on your way to all the love, passion, and adventure of times gone by!

HISTORICAL *Tapestry* ROMANCES

Silhouette Desire
15-Day Trial Offer

A new romance series that explores contemporary relationships in exciting detail

Six Silhouette Desire romances, free for 15 days!
We'll send you six new Silhouette Desire romances to look over for 15 days, absolutely free! If you decide not to keep the books, return them and owe nothing.

Six books a month, free home delivery. If you like Silhouette Desire romances as much as we think you will, keep them and return your payment with the invoice. Then we will send you six new books every month to preview, just as soon as they are published. You pay only for the books you decide to keep, and you never pay postage and handling.